INOCULUM

◆ FriesenPress

Suite 300 - 990 Fort St
Victoria, BC, V8V 3K2
Canada

www.friesenpress.com

Copyright © 2020 by Archie Alafriz
First Edition — 2020

ISBN
978-1-5255-6853-4 (Hardcover)
978-1-5255-6854-1 (Paperback)
978-1-5255-6855-8 (eBook)

1. FICTION, CRIME

Distributed to the trade by The Ingram Book Company

INOCULUM

a novel by

ARCHIE ALAFRIZ

Dedicated to my lovely wife

A special salute to all COVID-19 front line workers.
Thank you for your immense courage.

THE BALOCH

It was 4:03 a.m. in Vancouver. Everyone was tired and tempers were short. The task force had been on two South Asian targets for the past 46 hours. No one on the investigative team had slept the past two nights and I was at my breaking point. I was so tired that I was having auditory hallucinations.

The surveillance teams, on the other hand, worked rotating shifts, providing 24/7 coverage for an entire week. They were relieved by an incoming shift every 10 hours. They were not investigative teams; they were vigilant eyes and ears. They collected evidence at times, but their job was to report what their targets did during their shift. Surveillance objectives often varied; sometimes it was as loose as observing the lifestyles of the targets. Sometimes it was specific, like collecting cast-off DNA from a discarded cup of coffee. They called out the movements of the targets about town, vehicles they drove, meetings they made, and transactions they conducted.

We were all surveillance trained, but there are teams that do this kind of thing on a full-time basis. Personally, I would only use these specialized teams because if you haven't done it in a while, well, it's a perishable skill. And I have seen real keystone-cop knucklehead shit out there.

At midnight, the surveillance team handed over control of the targets to the investigative team. That meant that the surveillance team would be disengaging and that we, the investigators, would be taking over. This usually happens while the target is static. A handover is not something you want to do on the move.

My task force belonged to the Integrated National Security Enforcement Team, or INSET. It was conceived in principle the very day the World Trade Centre towers and the Pentagon were attacked that fateful 11th day of September, 2001. We were the anti-terrorist police, working for the National Security Program of the Royal Canadian Mounted Police, Canada's federal police force whose authorities and jurisdictions were similar to those of its better-known counterpart and agency partner, the FBI. Our integrated units across the Great White North were the Canadian equivalent of the Department of Homeland Security. And since 9-11, our unit's main focus had been Sunni extremism. In this, and all our other investigations, we prioritized the identification of Sunni extremists, neutralized the threat if it existed, recommended criminal charges if that avenue was available, and then forged on to the next case. For the past decade and a half, this was our cookie-cutter response to radicalization.

The plan for this night was to hit an apartment unit in a high-rise building before daybreak. The apartment tenants had also rented a storage room in the basement of the building. The search warrant covered both these locations. And we had permission from the judge to execute the warrant by night to preserve the integrity of the investigation as well as avail the best chances of preserving evidence. We did not seek permission to forego the requirement of announcing police presence before the hard entry. The apartment was only 760 square feet and the assault team figured it could cover that area in a few seconds.

This investigation had begun a month before when a confidential informant tipped off the police that these two targets supplied precursor chemicals to a clan lab on the North Shore, and that this was the work of a Middle Eastern Organized Crime (MEOC) group that traffics in MDMA globally (most people know MDMA by its street name, Ecstasy). There was previous but outdated intelligence on this South Asian duo; they were already known to the police. Their blotter said that they supplied at least two of the nine-plus precursor chemicals needed to make Ecstasy. That info came from another investigation in Alberta. The info was passed on to the police in Vancouver, but like a substantial amount of intelligence data, it fell on deaf ears. The intel also said that the duo was tightly connected with a commercial supplier who shipped pseudo ephedrine and caffeine from Ontario. The rest of the clan lab chemicals were supplied to the crime group by other players. This operation was a wide mix of ethnicities strewn together for a common criminal purpose.

For the very first time, my task force would be going head to head with this MEOC group. A handful of its players were known to us, but at that time, we only had mostly uncorroborated intelligence. These individuals had had innocuous brushes with uniformed patrol officers, but beyond that, there wasn't much else on them, no convictions of any kind.

I had long suspected that the North Shore crime group was associated to, if not directly controlled by, Hezbollah. It was a brave claim, I know. It was pretty brazen, actually; I was the only investigator to ever bring this up. The problem was, while everyone around me relied solely on criminal intelligence, my deductions flowed from financial intelligence. People around me joked that it was the equivalent of voodoo. But I was certain that night that my team had never been so close to taking down the Ayatollah's henchmen.

We'd had our analysts busy piecing together the target profiles for the team over the previous week. We were initially surprised to learn that our two targets were not actually Middle Eastern; based on their group profile, the analysts identified their ethnicity as South Asian, specifically, Baloch.

I distinctly recall Googling this word on my workstation (and I recall barely being able to read the screen from fatigue). I'd like to think that I am fairly well travelled, but until then, I had never even come across the term. The first hit was a Wiki definition: *Balochistan*, it said, *is the largest province in Pakistan, bordering Iran to the west and Afghanistan to the north.* I had scrambled to find out more about the Baloch people.

We had been monitoring the targets' cellular traffic for a week. We soon learned that this investigation was going to present a language translation nightmare from the outset. The recordings sounded like we'd captured all the languages of middle earth. Some of the recognizable ones were Dari, Pashtun, and Urdu. But Balochi? We had no translator for the Balochi dialect. We were told that, depending on their hometown's distance from the Iranian border, there was likelihood that the Baloch could speak Dari. We needed to know this in case we needed to communicate with them in any language other than English. Our Canada Border Services Agency (CBSA) coordinator learned that there were only 11 Baloch families on the West Coast. Their immigration documents indicated that they were all from the same village, and that they had all been sponsored by the same individual, meaning that they were likely all blood relatives. This would make finding an independent translator difficult, if not impossible.

A voice crackled over the encrypted radio. It was the team commander (TC) transmitting from the mobile command centre. We had started using digitally encrypted radios over a decade ago. They are a godsend. Being virtually secure, our operations security was assured. Because we no longer really need to use cryptic language or 10-codes of old, we can actually communicate in plain English. Being able to communicate with greater depth of context can actually stave off disaster.

"Heads up, gals," the TC intoned. "The warrant is on site. ERT is on pre-breach briefing. We are going kinetic in a few minutes.

If you have any reason to enter the premises, please read and initial the warrant here at the MCC and don't forget to sign-in and sign-out of the log." This told me that the investigator who had obtained the search warrant had now arrived at the scene. The kick-in was now imminent.

My name is Alec Alton. I am a constable—it's the lowest designation in this 13-rank organization. It is also the most important one. I am the most senior constable in my unit and the most experienced. Where the rubber meets the road, I command more respect and more allegiance from the people I work with than the commissioner. That's just the way it works. I joined the RCMP to be right where I am, here in national security, working the trenches and protecting my country. I didn't come to this job to manage or supervise people. I decided that a long time ago. I am here to physically remove the threats, because those folks with the letters behind their names—PhD, MA, MBA, whatever—ain't gonna do that for you. They call on me and my ilk to do that.

When people ask me what my work is like, I tell them that if James Bond's job was real, mine was the closest thing to it. And, as I recall, Agent 007 was a tad dissentient. Well, that's me too. But I'm not so much anti-management (I do like my superiors at a personal level) as I am anti-establishment. I love the RCMP but deplore the institutionalized thinking. So no, I don't always get along with the suits. But I bring the bad guys in. They don't. To borrow from the famously misquoted prose of Richard Grenier: "We sleep soundly in our beds because rough men stand ready in the night to visit violence upon those who would do us harm." I am, proudly, one of those rough men. And I will gladly visit violence upon those who deserve it.

For that particular night's operation, the team had decided to use the Vancouver Police Emergency Response Team, or Vancouver ERT. That's a SWAT team to the uninitiated. Working with specialist teams brings a whole new set of dynamics to the operation. It's like a complex surgery, where specialists gather around the operating table, efficiently complete the task that needs to get done, and then simply disperse when it's all done. As Vancouver ERT is much more familiar with the neighbourhoods here than RCMP ERT is, we requested Vancouver's finest to help us out.

Upon hearing that we were on countdown to hard entry, I ran up the fire exit stairwell of an adjacent building and entered an apartment unit directly across the street from the targets' building. As I walked into the living room, I noticed an elderly lady sleeping on a chesterfield with two blankets over her. *Poor lady*, I thought. The building on the west side was predominantly occupied by retirees, and this lady had given the police permission to use her home for this operation.

The elderly woman propped herself up when she detected my presence. She mumbled something about offering me tea, God bless her. But I lightly touched her arm and asked her not to bother. We'd inconvenienced her enough. She just smiled and slid back down under her comforter.

I glanced over toward the open patio door when I felt the cool chill of fresh ocean air. I could see a figure in the darkness, crouched in position with his rifle resting on a padded bench. This was the Vancouver ERT sniper. I approached the window, being cognizant of where the natural light emanated from. I needed to make sure I didn't backlight his position. I nodded at him as he gently lifted a finger off the scope he was adjusting, acknowledging my presence. Snipers are a different bunch; this holds true for the police just as it does for the military. Two words define them: focus and patience. And the snipers I know are quiet and sometimes distant. Go figure.

From his perch, the sniper had an unobstructed view of the seventh floor window and patio door of the targets' apartment. The targets lived in a middle unit flanked by two other balconies on either side. I mentally confirmed that it was the correct target apartment as described on the file. It was game time. Everyone had their game faces on. No unnecessary talking, no pleasantries, and certainly no unnecessary movements.

Standing beside the sniper, manning a spotting scope, was a fellow I recognized as my buddy and teammate Isaac Renner. He was a young constable who was new to national security, but long on maturity and operational with-it-ness. He gave me a low and slow five just before I turned to show myself out of the apartment. Renner was not only our spotter; he was also invaluable for his familiarity with the targets. He could identify them and call their movements over the radio. And, perhaps more importantly, he could also identify non-targets, in case there were other people in the apartment that the surveillance team had not accounted for. Shit like that always happens; it's just Murphy's Law.

In the minutes before all hell breaks loose, there is always a distinct moment of eerie stillness. You can feel it in the air, and also perceive it over the police radio—a restless silence. Whatever it is, it can be cut with a knife.

It was now 4:40 a.m. Dawn was breaking over the scenic city. To the north, I could see the North Shore Mountains silhouetted by the impending sunrise. Oddly, I don't recall hearing any birds that morning. It was like the calm before the storm, the stillness in the woods before a tsunami hits, the hush before an earthquake. I made it back to the ground floor and pushed the crash bars of the fire exit that led me back to the street. I stood off to one side of the plaza in front of the targets' building. I looked around my surroundings for a minute. I knew that there were over 30 police officers involved in this operation—yet from where I stood, and from most other vantage points around the block, no one else could be seen.

Just then, I heard a pre-amp microphone click on over my ear-piece. A second later, the voice of TC calmly informed us, "Heads up, all units. Control has been handed over to the Vancouver ERT commander. Comms is with ERT dispatcher… Timer set for five… Steady up."

It felt like forever, but suddenly a muffled voice could be heard. This one wasn't coming from the radio; it came from somewhere in the distance, out in the night. "Police! Search warrant." This was followed by a tangible shudder emanating from the outer walls of the targets' building—it had clearly been a pretty hard entry. I looked up toward the seventh-floor balconies, but they were on the wrong side of daybreak. It was still night on the targets' side of the structure. In my tired mind's eye, I imagined the suspects at that very moment, being overwhelmed by surprise and the speed of the onslaught. They always are.

Then my mind auto-flipped back to task. Evidence would need to be collected during the search of the apartment. I hopped over a bush to retrieve exhibit bags from my unmarked police car parked across the side street. I heard Renner's voice over the radio. "They're out on the balcony. Stand by—they're down."

A tired mind processes everything more slowly. *What do you mean, 'they're down?'* By this time, I had walked past the corner of the building, behind a wide pillar. I can't recall what I heard first—Renner's voice, or the loud, sickening, almost metallic sound of two bodies impacting the stone slabs of the plaza floor. It took a good second before my mind put it together. The radio was silent for what seemed like an eternity. With concerted effort, I turned around and ran back towards the plaza, past the wide pillar.

All I could see in the low light were two blurs on the ground. Police officers were running in from all different directions, converging on these blurs. Beams of high intensity flashlights sawed through the darkness. I walked over to one of the bodies, lying still on the ground. There was no way to identify which target was which. No clothing descriptions had been given during the briefing. One body was still emitting a burbling sound, the sound of life gurgling down a vacuous drain. Someone in the group said, "Take a dying declaration." Everyone looked at him incredulously. I felt a loud thrumming in my ears, and then I realized it was my own heart pumping, like I had just run a marathon.

The TC came back over the air. "Hold stations, we have an in-custody death situation. Oscar Charlie is advised, and the coroner will be summoned at daylight. ERT team can stand down. Supervisors, identify your personnel for critical incident debriefing. Secure the apartment. Lock down the plaza."

I ran toward the side of the building and grabbed the fire exit door handle just as it opened. There was Renner, carrying down his gear. He was visibly shaken and obviously in a state of disbelief. He looked at me with a half-exasperated, half-confused look.

"What the fuck happened?" I asked. "Were there shots fired?" I hadn't heard any shots ring out.

"Hell, no," Renner replied. "Dude, it was like, ERT hit the door, and these guys joined up on the balcony, climbed over the railing, grabbed each other, and fell. Maybe they jumped? There was no time for anyone to react." By his account, Renner couldn't tell if the targets had fallen or jumped to their deaths. And only he and the sniper had had an eye on them during their final moments.

Tunnel vision is a real phenomenon. It affects recollections of witnesses because, in their recount, there is always some data omitted. The narrowing of perception allows our minds to peripherally discard sensory inputs. That's a physiological fight-or-flight response. As apex predators, humans need to constantly train against millions of years of evolutionary genetic instructions. Eight years ago, for example, a man with a knife advanced on me outside of his home. The man had just stabbed his wife several times and slit her throat. As soon as my partner and I arrived on the scene, he came running out of his suite and attacked two other police officers who had arrived to back us up. So there were three other officers within several meters of me. We were all shouting commands to the man to drop his knife. When he lunged at one of the officers, I fired one shot despite being in a cross-fire situation. I needed to stop him before he killed one of us. But, amid the mayhem, no one heard the shot that I fired—not even me. I only confirmed to myself that I had fired the shot because

I saw the muzzle flash come from my pistol. The open line to the 911 call-taker recorded the loud pistol report, clear as day, despite the complainant's hand phone being inside the home at the time of the shooting. But, for us officers out on the scene, it took time to realize that the knife-wielding suspect had been shot right in front of us, and to respond appropriately with first aid. This is why it is important to note down your own observations immediately, and separately from everyone else.

By 6:30 a.m., I had finished securing the target residence with yellow tape, and had stickered and initialed the door. Then my thoughts immediately turned to the beckoning call of my bed. It had been 48 hours since I had last seen my bed, and there was nothing else I could competently accomplish at that time, anyway. Everyone else needed to debrief at the Vancouver City Police headquarters ten minutes away. I decided to contact the TC, whom I had previously worked for during my uniform days on patrol. Calling from my police-issued smartphone, I dialled the mobile command centre.

"Kenney," I said. "This is the last time I work a project with you, you bastard. You got that Midas touch, you know. Except everything you touch turns to shit. In this case, it's dead. Which is shit."

Kenney chuckled. "Did I ever tell you, lad, that working for you—"

"—'is more fun than pitch-forking babies?'" I finished off his sentence. "Yeah, yeah, yeah." That was his favourite quip to me, but only me. He had first said that to me when I was a recruit on my field training 27 years ago. I didn't know what to make of it back then. A quarter of a century later, it had become our favourite term of endearment.

"Get your ass to bed," he said. "I'll call out your evening crew."

"Copy that," I replied. "I also need peeps for site security. So, Ident, the coroner, and, oh, a couple members for the autopsies." We refer to ourselves as "members"—we're all members of Club Fed, the

RCMP. I wondered if I was missing anything else. I was just so tired.

"Yeah, yeah, get the fuck outta here," Kenney repeated. He knew this drill better than anyone.

"Thanks, staff. By the way, don't stand down the Hazmat team yet. God knows what we'll find up there this afternoon," I said as I walked toward my car.

"Don't worry, I'll call the CD myself," Kenney replied. The CD is the Vancouver Police Chief Dispatcher, our conduit to their agency. The CD also supervises all the calls dispatched to their zone or district units. If we ever have to come into Vancouver for work, it is imperative that the CD knows we've come into their jurisdiction. This mitigates potential gunplay between agencies of different jurisdictions, a situation known as friendly fire. In reality, it's just etiquette.

Thank God for Kenney. I hung up and headed to my PC, my unmarked police cruiser. All I could think about was my bed.

BEAUTY AND THE BRAIN

The suspects' names were Adham and Armaan Baloch, brothers, 27 and 25
years old, respectively. Or at least that's what their passports said. I
found those in their apartment as I walked in the door later that day.

As the exhibit custodian, my job was to direct the search team
toward the types of evidence the investigators were looking for. The
search team then identifies the materials for seizure and I document
the items' original locations, and record which officer found them
and the time and dates they were located. I then physically seize the
exhibits and take them into my custody.

Before disturbing anything, I took some time to look around the
apartment first. Earlier, one of the search team members had taken a
video to document the pre-search condition of the apartment. The
video would not only give me an account of the location of the
items as they lay, but would also document what exhibits were in
plain view.

The apartment could be described as spartan. The neighbourhood
inquiry conducted that morning had confirmed that this was, in fact,
the residence of the Baloch brothers. But the apartment featured
only the barest of necessities. There were mattresses on the floor,
two prayer mats, a Quran, some dishes, and some scattered articles of
clothing. Everything suggested that they were prepared to skip town
at a moment's notice.

Both were Canadian citizens; they were both issued Canadian

passports. They had resided locally for the past five years. Adham was married. I found a copy of a family sponsorship application for his wife and two small children who were residing in Quetta, the provincial capital of Balochistan, while waiting for their sponsorship to go through. My mind raced forward to the NOK, the notification to the next of kin. If the kin were in a foreign land, who would we get to deliver the bad news? *I'll deal with that later*, I thought. Unlike Adham, Armaan was single. But because they were brothers, one NOK would suffice. I would need to locate local relatives, if they had any. Otherwise, I would have to put in a request to the International Operations Branch in Ottawa to locate and advise the family in Quetta. We have liaison officers (LOs) all over the world.

I looked up upon hearing Corporal Ameena al-Amine, our terrorist finance expert, walk into the apartment and scrawl her name into the entry logbook that had been placed by the door. In Arabic, her name means justice and trustworthiness; I am told that the prophet Muhammad was called al-Amine in his youth. Ameena was a bit of an enigma in the force. She was supremely intelligent and extremely competent—but, as is often the case, her head-turning beauty often got in the way of her getting recognized for those other qualities. In her late 40's, she was still in the prime of her beauty, gorgeous without knowing it (how rare is that?). Sadly, though, some people never actually got past her appearance to see the other things she brought to the table.

She was born in Morocco, to a French-Moroccan father and a Scandinavian mother. The mixing of these bloodlines had resulted in the best possible combination in her. Ameena came from pedigree as well; her grandfather was a retired member of the Supreme Council of the Judiciary, which is presided over by the King of Morocco. Her father was an international law professor at the University of British Columbia. Her mother was a freelance writer/journalist and food critic, but more significantly, she was only one of four master sommeliers in Canada. This was how Ameena was afforded a Swiss education. In Geneva, she had picked up an impressive collection of languages: French, Italian, German, and Spanish. And this was in addition to the two other languages she already spoke with equal fluency, English and Arabic.

Ameena was one of those enlightened souls, born with a well-developed sense of reason, aptitude, and fairness. Despite being an only child (and likely spoiled by doting parents), she was the living embodiment of Justitia, Lady Justice (in fact, I think she might have been a Libra, too). She was all about defending those who could not defend themselves. And it had nothing to do with a superhero complex; it was simply what she had been born to do, and what she had gravitated toward in spite of so many other more prestigious career opportunities open to her.

I first worked with her during our junior days in uniform. She proved herself to be one hell of a street cop. She was absolutely fearless, unafraid to get down and dirty when she had to, mixing it up in one of the toughest cities to police in the country. She was great backup at any fracas, busting skull like the best of them.

The men on the watch looked up to her and even sought her out for investigative advice because she was strong in her knowledge of the law. In her career, she was already responsible for two vital case laws. Both were the first-of-their-kind criminal charges laid in the Supreme Court of British Columbia: the first was a charge of terrorist fundraising in Canada, a piece of legislation that came into law after 9-11; the second had to do with properly securing digital evidence obtained from the Internet. She had the innate ability to predict legal hurdles early in the investigative process, often ahead of the crown attorneys. And her cases were ingeniously constructed. She was an incredible team leader and primary investigator. There was a long list of members waiting eagerly for the chance to be chosen for her next project team.

Personally, I liked her because she was real and down to earth. She always remained eagle-eye focused on the job at hand, and kept everyone on their toes. I always appreciated her presence because she brightened up the room and everyone's moods (of course, no one wanted her around at parties— kicking back, getting stupid, and showing your goofy side becomes a hell of a lot more awkward when you're around someone you respect to the point of intimidation). That being said, there was also the sense that a part of her was always withdrawn and somewhat distant. It's been that way ever since her husband died. He had been a member of JTF2, Canada's lesser known version of a highly specialized military unit, the equivalent of the US Delta Force or the British SAS. After 9-11, JTF2 inserted itself into the Afghan Northern Alliance, and Ameena's husband was killed during a classified mission. She never spoke about it.

Ameena and I have been friends for a long time. I keep her secrets, and she keeps mine. I was always glad when we wound up on a case together, because there was always something I could learn from her, whether it be a new investigative technique, a new approach, new tech, or just a new mindset—people could live off her refuse. And it was always serious fun working with her, because she was able get deep into new and challenging situations.

As I continued snooping around the apartment, I came upon some granular powder. I guessed it was red phosphorus. I was looking up the handling instructions for the chemical when the rest of the search team arrived. They entered the apartment and signed the log. All of a sudden, the place became very crowded. There was a stack of manila envelopes containing documents piled up by the fireplace. The heap caught Ameena's eye and she made a beeline toward it. She noted that one of the picture frames mounted on the wall was off-kilter, just a bit off-square. It was a religious picture of sorts.

"Someone please strip the frame," she said to no one in particular as she made her way to the fireplace.

I was the closest person to the photograph so I unhooked it off the wall. Initially, I looked behind the frame and saw nothing unusual. There were layers of cardboard backing, which is usual, although it looked thicker than normal. I undid all the clips and the cardboard layers started coming apart. And, sure enough, sandwiched between the photograph and the cardboard were several sheets of carefully laid-out Amex traveller's cheques. I called for someone to hand me the DSLR camera. After taking a few shots, I started counting the cheques. They were all in $500 USD denominations. There were 62 cheques totalling $31,000 USD.

Other than the red phosphorus, a two-gram clump of what looked like black (Afghan) heroin, and the cheques, there was nothing else of interest from a national security perspective. There were no books, notes, flags, videos, or other evidence of extremist activity. Ameena got up with the manila envelopes clutched in her hand and yelled, "Okay, guys, VPD confirmed that they'll handle the sudden death. We're just doing nexus to terrorism, so if we can't find it, we're out of here. We'll hand it off to drugs."

I was curious about the traveller's cheques and where the suspects had intended to go. But for now, I only needed to bag and tag all exhibits and pack them up for transport.

"See you all back at the barn. And don't forget to log out of the scene and seize the log before leaving," Ameena continued. She walked over to the kitchen and placed a call to Kenney. "Staff," she said, "we're gonna clear. We're taking a few hard drives with us and some documents, but for the most part, this location is sanitized. I got a call from the morgue and there were a couple of cell phones recovered with the bodies. I'll have those picked up and brought down to ITCU. Meantime," she continued, "we'll lock the place down and hand it over to drugs."

"Sounds good," said Kenney. I could hear him over the speaker. "Let me know ahead of time if you need anything else. Let's not do last minute shit," Kenney added before ending the call.

Ameena walked over to me and said, "Look at these. These are copies of their last year's tax returns. The brothers operated a janitorial service business which employs 40 people. I bet you that's 40 straw employees. That's a hell of a shell company. And there's another book here. I gather from these repeating values that they made their money from only two types of precursor chemical shipments. These bank statements show they received drafts from a local casino, and the dates coincide with the dates on these waybills—they're all exactly two days apart. Also, look at the company's bank cheque stubs. They're all still in the booklet. These guys moved $600,000 in revenue last year. And that's just what they declared. They have no payroll. Look around, what do you see?"

I scanned the apartment again, even though I'd just inventoried everything in it. Six hundred large can buy a lot of luxury. I've executed search warrants on the most lavishly appointed homes of drug dealers, and you can instantly tell what they spend their money on. But here, in this hole-in-the-wall flat located in a rough West End neighbourhood, these guys owned nothing. There were two rooms, one and a half baths, and a couch that looked like it was repossessed from a dumpster. There were two prayer mats. They did not even own proper beds. They slept on foam mattresses placed directly on the floor. There was hardly any food in the fridge, no alcohol. Other than a few religious items and a hookah, the place was bare. *Forget not having cable—how could they not even have a TV?* I wondered idly. There is a saying in jihad: "A bullet wasted is a bullet a brother in battle goes without."

"I'm taking a few of these discs and all the hard drives," I told Ameena.

"Sure," she said. "Get a 1474 down to ITCU to mirror the originals; we need an analysis of the metadata. Make two copies for disclosure, please. Also, two extra mirror images, one for us and another for the drug section. If these guys were any good, they obfuscated the destinations of their funds, or transferred them manually using traveller's cheques. We have no suspects to interview, now that the ones we had in-hand conveniently decided to check out. We can't establish a terrorism nexus if we can't link them directly to any ideology. Otherwise, they're just drug dealers.

"The best scenario," she continued, "is that we find a money trail leading us to terrorists. Then we can have ourselves a financial investigation." Ameena beamed with excitement at the prospect of tracing money. She made me laugh sometimes. It's good work, but I don't get excited over it.

Back in the office, I wrote out the analysis request for ITCU and sent it along with the original discs. I secured those in the ITCU temporary exhibit lockers. ITCU is the Integrated Technical Crimes Unit. Think of it as a geek squad—with guns. Normally, they attend the search sites, but I called them off this one because there just wasn't enough space in the apartment for them and their portable extraction gear. And unlike mirroring computers at a business where the computers are still in use, the seizure of these ones wouldn't inconvenience anyone. Not the Baloch brothers anyway. And the ITCU members were happy not to drive the 32 miles through rush hour traffic from their office to get to the search site. Instead of ITCU extracting data from the computers and drives *in situ*, I seized the computers the old school way and brought them back to headquarters for forensic examination.

Nowadays, ITCU has become an indispensable support unit involved in nearly all types of criminal investigations. It is a culture of extremely helpful individuals all too often overwhelmed by the amount of work on their plates. Soon, this unit will be the spearhead of investigations instead of its shaft. It would be in everyone's interest to fund ITCU units so that they can advance their technologies ahead of criminal tech. A large fraction of frauds, thefts, ransoms, blackmails, intimidations, bullying, and extortions are perpetrated online. Even those crimes that don't rely on tech platforms to commit the actual offence might use online pay systems to move money, cryptocurrency, or other informal value like iTunes credit. Today, FinTech are the movers and shakers. Police forces traditionally train in rearward-looking processes. Their managers need to cultivate a culture outside of the institutionalized think. They need a unit that can harness the power of big data to create predictive models to scale future policing needs and scope necessary modifications to its architecture. Soon, the police will be saturated into ineffectiveness. They're pretty much already there.

With sterile copies of the drives at hand, I picked one of them to view. The first drive contained home videos of Adham Baloch. He must have taken this video the last time he went home. According to his passport, he was last home in August 2018. The last stamp on his passport was Pakistan. Between the entry and departure dates were exactly 14 days. I gathered that these were recent videos taken by a video camera. Most people just use their phones nowadays. The files were arranged into a proprietary format like a DVD, complete with a menu. The disc opened to a scene selection page, with five scene thumbnails. I clicked on the first thumbnail, which opened to a family picnic scene. Here were what appeared to be Baloch people engaged in their typical recreation. There was a family walking along a very rocky road, headed towards a rocky riverbank. They all picked a rock to sit on, laid out their food, and tucked in. Later, the kids played on the rocks while some of the adult males bathed in a rocky pool fed by the river. There were no GPS tags to the videos, but I knew that the Quetta area has many rivers and lakes, particularly to the west of Hazarganji-Chiltan National Park. My thoughts turned to the fact that Adham would never be returning home. This family that I was watching would never realize its Canadian dream. The young kids would never see their father again. I clicked on each of the other thumbnails, but the videos were all the same.

I looked at all the other drives. They were more of the same: family photos, copies of immigration documents, and screen captures of Adham's blogs on a Balochi language website. Later in the week I had an Urdu translator go over whatever sections of the blogs he could understand, but nothing of evidentiary value was found. It left me wondering who Adham and Armaan Baloch really were. What were they doing with the money they raised? Were they an operational cell? A funding cell? For whom, and who were their local associates?

The next day, Ameena approached my workstation. She had already recovered two cell phones from the morgue and had them triaged on Cellbrite software. Adham and Armaan were each carrying one when they fell. Or jumped.

"We did the phone data dump this morning," she said. "There weren't a lot of names on their contact lists. The sim cards are both foreign. And the only regular calls they made on those phones were to Pakistan. We checked the 92-country code and 81 city routing, and those came back to the city of Quetta. We went through their contact lists, GPS-photo logs, and recent travel history. Only one thing of interest showed up."

I let her continue. My brain was still stuck on how nice she smelled that morning, and every morning. All the time. I suppose she noticed that I was somewhat distracted; she slapped a piece of paper onto my desk and gently nudged me on the back of the head to look at the document.

"Look, I rushed this request to CBSA. These are their travel history printouts. Intel only, pending the Privacy Act request. This name here, Nasser Tushanni, his number is the only one they commonly called. And the calls recur frequently and regularly. So, I also asked for Nasser Tushanni's travel history. It showed Tushanni returning to Canada, via both YVR and Pearson, 17 times in the past 12 months. I'm rushing a voluntary information request for financial data today. I won't get the report for a couple of weeks but the analyst in Ottawa pulled some raw numbers for me already. She told me over the phone that Tushanni declares several hundred thousand in US dollars almost every other time he returns to Canada from Afghanistan."

That last part sparked my attention and woke me from my Ameena stupor. "Several hundred grand?" I asked.

"Yeah, he declared all of them on his entry statutory declaration form," she said. "He told CBSA that he had been liquidating property in Afghanistan."

"So, he paid taxes on that money?" I asked, incredulous.

"You would think so. Declaring the funds to customs doesn't mean he declares them to the taxman. They're two different things. I know that Canada Revenue Agency does check with FINTRAC but only when there is already an investigation. There's so much raw data out there, no one has a grasp on what they mean. I gotta call someone. Later."

Ameena walked back towards her office.

Ameena's expertise was in terrorist finance. She had explained to me that these "global compliance regimes" were initially designed to address money laundering. Then, almost as an afterthought after 9-11, they piled on new reporting requirements for terrorist financing. But platforms like FINTRAC were created with anti-money laundering architecture. Terrorist financing is a totally different thing. She said that the best analogy was like using a mouse trap to capture gerbils; wrong concept, wrong design. She said that in tracking seven terrorist organizations that raised funds in Canada, none of them ever laundered money. Therefore, they did not trigger any of the money laundering indicators FINTRAC was looking for.

Only Ameena seemed confident about advancing terrorism investigations. She didn't baulk at the technical stuff. She savoured it. I have no idea where she learned her stuff or what she read for that matter.

One day, over morning coffee, she tried to explain it to me and Renner. I believe the greatest virtue of a teacher is the ability to dumb down complex topics to their simplest elements. That takes real mastery. So, over a cup of java, Ameena laid it on us. She said: "Look, you guys have taken your Proceeds of Crime course, right? All compliance regimes start with the money laundering model. This consists of the placement, the layering, and the integration indicators."

In other words, the way bad guys wash dirty money is by first plunking the money down on something, say, a printing press business. Then they layer the money stream by purchasing and reselling services, inventory, etc. But, ultimately, the money is integrated back into the bad guy's control through means like real estate, where the bad guy now owns a mansion. His wealth looks like it was legitimately earned. So, all those analysts in the financial intel units are trained to detect these three indicators in sequence. There are secondary indicators, of course, but everything is about those three primary indicators. Intrinsically, this is nothing but a process-driven system. It's kind of binary. It's there or it's not there.

Terrorist financing, Ameena went on to explain, is a totally different animal. The difference, in principle, is that most terrorist money is legally obtained. It comes from contributions, or a person's own wages or investments, sales of assets, etc. So logically, there is no reason to launder ostensibly clean money. That's why, most of the time, you can't expect to see any money laundering indicators when terrorist finances are transacted through the financial systems. And more importantly, unlike normal criminality where the bad guy needs to bring this wealth back under his control through, say, an asset—car, boat, or mansion—terrorist money is immediately spent on operations. It is never amassed in static wealth because there is never enough of it. Terrorist financing can't simply be reduced to indicators. So the process-based approach just won't work. We need real financial *intelligence*, not just black-and-white financial data. The data needs to be accompanied by intimate knowledge of risks in the region—essentially, it must work in tandem with a regional threat matrix.

"Okay, Ameena," I said. "That's it. Let's go back upstairs." So much for coffee-time small talk. It was always work-work-work with Ameena; she was never one to engage in idle banter. I wondered what she talked about at home. That being said, I certainly appreciated everything I learned when working with her. It just took me a while to digest so much information.

FROM US ONE, WITH LOVE

The following week, I headed over to the Intelligence Team. The people who work there collect and analyze criminal intelligence that has a nexus to terrorism. The team members do not work cases themselves; instead, they monitor various individuals or groups for targeting purposes. Depending on a combination of threat level and urgency, they recommend unit priorities for enforcement action.

Sergeant Ian Tibbs was a corpulent guy. He never moved too quickly in any one direction, which was all right with me because it meant I never had to walk far to find him. It was a short distance between his office and the kitchenette. Ian was the unit conduit to our intelligence partners. He kept track of who sat at which intelligence desk and what expertise the partner agencies could bring to bear on our investigation. Ian was what we call a re-thread, someone from another police agency who transferred over to the Mounties. In his case, he was a Norwich cop, but before that, he served in the British armed forces. Ian was SAS, no less. And yes, there was a time when he was lean and mean. There was a framed photograph on a filing cabinet behind his desk that featured him, shirtless and chiseled, in front of a downed Argentine F1 Mirage fighter jet during the battle of the Falklands. But clearly, his Rambo days were long past him. Today, this man's hulk was equaled only by his gentlemanly behaviour, sincerity, and intelligence. He was really a very nice man, a decorated British hero, and a wizard of anything and everything.

"Sarge," I called out from the doorway of his office. "Can I ask you to check with US One on a subject? This is on that file with the two jumpers last week."

"Come in, lad," he said.

I took another step closer but remained on the threshold to make it clear that I didn't intend to stay. His office was adorned with military and cop paraphernalia and mementos. He had the usual collectibles in there: hats, badges, medals, and certificates. All those are relatively common to keep in an office; but he also kept curious items, like a deactivated grenade launcher. He even had an array of different mortar rounds lined up according to size. I imagined that if his office were any larger, he would have probably parked a portable MANPAD anti-aircraft missile launcher in there, like a Stinger (he actually had one, in his garage at home).

US One was our nomenclature for the CIA, thanks to Ian. He believed that after 9-11, the CIA's existence was doomed, and that the agency would be renamed because of its failure to prevent the attacks on the WTC and the Pentagon. So Ian took it upon himself to rename it "US One" ahead of time. I don't know where he pulled that name out of, but we kept the nickname to appease him. I wondered what he would name his dog if he had one. It became a name we bandied about inside intelligence circles.

"Nasser Tushanni," I said to Ian. "I have the DOB at my desk. He's about 68 years, Afghan. I've got further identifiers. I'll encrypt them over to you."

"You betcha, mate," Ian replied, and with a nod, I headed back out. I was confident that Ian was going to get on it right away by making two phone calls, the first to US One, and the second to his spook buddies at the British Embassy in Ottawa. That would be the SIS, the Secret Intelligence Service (better known to most, as James Bond's MI6).

I suspect the intelligence community created the word *deconfliction*. It doesn't even sound like a proper word. But it is a necessary process undertaken by various agencies to ensure that they do not interfere with each other's covert operations. It is particularly important to deconflict with the 5 Eyes (or FVEY) with whom Canada is a signatory, the alliance of Australia, the United Kingdom, the United States of America, Canada, and New Zealand. It is a multilateral agreement on intelligence sharing: signals intelligence (SIGINT), military intelligence, and human intelligence (HUMINT). It's an older doctrine compared to more recent multilateral agreements, like that of the Egmont Group, a sharing agreement of financial intelligence (FININT) by 164 signatory financial intelligence units.

In Canada, national security is the responsibility of two organizations with distinctly different mandates. The RCMP collect criminal intelligence and conduct criminal investigations. The Canadian Security Intelligence Service (CSIS) collects security intelligence and reports this intelligence to the Government of Canada. Prior to 1984, the RCMP Security Service conducted national security investigations alone. In the spirit of cooperation, the RCMP shares criminal intelligence with CSIS. Conversely, when CSIS happens upon criminal intelligence, it will share the information with the RCMP. However, CSIS will not share security intelligence with the RCMP. Security intelligence, depending on how it is obtained, generally does not meet criminal evidentiary standards and the assumption must be that it is not admissible in court. Intercept warrants obtained under the CSIS Act are granted to a lesser standard than what is accepted as reasonable grounds under the Criminal Code. Hence the RCMP is leery of security intelligence, as it has a capacity for contaminating criminal intelligence. So communication between these agencies has been limited to predetermined liaison channels at the HQ level. Three commissions of inquiry— MacKenzie, MacDonald, and Major (Air India)—spanning the past four decades, stand testament to these communication challenges. Difficulties aside, working with CSIS over the years gives one a sense of their people's commitment to the task. I loved the arguments we've had. Arguments are born of passion and the drive to protect

Canadians. Then everyone goes to lunch together as if nothing happened. There are never any hard feelings here.

I called our imbedded CBSA investigator, Connie Weathers.

"Connie. Hey, it's me," I said.

Connie was very much like me; we were both lifers in the industry. Her favourite description of national security was: *It's like hotel California. You can check out anytime you like, you just can't ever fucking leave.* I always imagine her with a cigar in her mouth whenever she says that. She was initially seconded to us from immigration intelligence. She was an analyst who grew out of Citizenship and Immigration Canada, which merged with Canada Customs in the mid-nineties to become CBSA. Connie was a petit blonde powerhouse. Hands down, she was the best intelligence analyst in her agency's arsenal, and I mean across the country. Her work product belied her cute appearance and pleasant demeanour. But she packed a punch—no, a wallop. She was an unassuming can of whoop-ass. Over the years, chauvinistic, narcissistic morons in my organization had tried to bully and intimidate her. Despite her sweet demeanour, that was something Connie was always ready for. She reminded me of an angler fish, the kind with the light bulb hanging from its head. The light attracts dumb-ass, unsuspecting wildlife directly into its mouth. I had seen Connie dispatch these idiots faster than week-old moldy bread. In our office, she was indispensable. It took a number of years for people to figure that out. CBSA operates under a different corporate culture than the RCMP. Connie's ability to navigate these perilous cultural tides was much sought after by National HQ heavies. My unit commander had her back. The deputy director of national security had her back. And I had her back.

"When CBSA receives our formal request, do you think you can brief the team on the Baloch and where they stand in terms of global terrorism?" I asked.

"Sure," Connie responded. "But give me a few days to put a report together. You owe me lunch."

"You got it," I said.

A week later, Ameena popped over to my desk. She had been digging stuff up on her own. A couple of months before, she had attended the FBI Academy in Quantico, Virginia, to train in cyber counterterrorism. She got all the awesome courses. In Quantico, she chummed up with an Afghan computer whiz kid who was teaching the course. The kid's name was Jabril Yusufzai, and he just happened to be the nephew of the governor of Kandahar. Jabril himself was a Canadian citizen, who had done his undergrad at Queens University in Kingston, Ontario. On a family visit to Kandahar, one of his uncle's American contacts connected him to US Special Forces in the area. They used him to interlace their SIGINT tech with the generationally archaic cell network in the Helmand province. This allowed the NSA to monitor all cellular communications in Afghanistan. The data was uplinked via satellite and processed back in the US where it was subjected to phrase and locational algorithms. Jabril wrote the software that allowed Predator and Global Hawk drones to capture the pings cellular phones made to their networks. An exploit in the cell networks allowed for the auto-triangulation of cell phone locations. The system provided the NSA with dynamic location tracking and analysis capabilities. It was a significant covert op by the CIA that provided the exploitive tech that unsuspecting US contractors delivered to Afghan Wireless, the local cellular provider. There were trojans written into the software so that it neatly networked into NSA systems without those niggling configuration problems.

Every firmware upgrade was synchronized with those of the NSA systems. The uplink to Afghansat 1 was so seamless that it would have been the envy of every spy agency in the world, had they known about it. Furthermore, the satellite had an extra capacity unknown to the provider. The headroom was allocated to piggyback encrypted US military theatre warfare data. This includes tactical imaging and measurements from the drones. Afghansat 1 renders precision strike capabilities beyond visual range (BVR). That means that, say, an aircraft flying beyond the horizon to the target can receive target coordinates and missile flight guidance from the satellite instead of an AWACS flying in the area. The firing solutions are relayed to the attack aircraft; all the pilot needs to do is launch the ordinance, even from as far away as the next time zone. "Fire and forget," the software will walk the missile into the target, making the necessary corrections along the way.

The CIA loved Jabril. He was just so talented and industrious. And he was humble, too; everyone loved that about him. Jabril was also well connected back home in Afghanistan. He had some real street smarts for someone who went to school in Canada at an early age. So it was actually US One that hired him to do some R&D stateside; he lived in New York. When Ameena met him, he was moonlighting at the FBI Academy, teaching during his spare time.

It was Jabril who told Ameena about the Tushanni family, whom he knew as common fixtures in the region. It turned out that Nasser Tushanni was Baloch and not Pashtun as his profile indicated. He was the son of a southern region warlord based out of Lashkar Gah. Nasser's father, Masub, controlled poppy farms from Baghran, which is located in the centre of Afghanistan, all the way down to the Pakistani border and slightly into Balochistan. It was rumored that both Masub and Nasser worked with the Americans during the Soviet occupation of Afghanistan, doing some kind of anti-communist resistance operation. According to Jabril, Masub still controlled the poppy there today, and Jabril suspected that Masub may be both allied with the Taliban and feared by them. Nobody messed with him. Even his uncle, the governor, walked on eggshells around Masub.

As Ameena briefed me on what she had learned from Jabril, she was abruptly interrupted by the shrill ringing of my desk phone. The call display said it was Ian Tibbs.

"Sarge," I said as I picked up the receiver.

"Is Ameena there with you"? Ian asked. "She's not at her desk."

"Yep, slumming in my pit. What you got?" I asked.

"Can you guys walk over? Word back from US One."

I grabbed Ameena for the short walk to Sergeant Tibbs' office.

"Sit down. Close the door," Ian barked as we walked through the door. He sounded exasperated.

"Here it is," he said. "According to a retired US One agent I know, your guy Nasser Tushanni worked for the Agency back in the seventies. He remembered the name because his colleagues were doing some in-region work in Central Asia under one of their NGOs. Although he never met Tushanni himself, he recalls other agents returning from the region bitching about Tushanni being downright treacherous. That's the only reason he remembered the name, he said. I wonder if it could be the same person. That's off the books, by the way, so don't put it in your notes. Because the official response from the Agency is that it had nothing on a Nasser Tushanni. They have no one by that name in their holdings. Sounds like a whitewash of some kind. I can't speculate why. I'll check with MI6. There might be a trace that migrated across the pond via FVEY channels that they forgot to scrub." He was referring to the fact that, sometimes, we share what is innocuous information at the time with our intelligence partners. Then, suddenly, the information later turns out to be *not* so innocuous and its too late to un-share it. It's kind of like an e-mail accidentally sent; you can't take it back.

"My buddy will do some digging and will let me know if anything more surfaces," Ian continued.

I noticed that Ameena didn't bring up the information she just got from Jabril. She kept her cards close to her chest. She was like that; she sat back and let the intel work itself through. This was the CIA we were talking about now, not the FBI whom we were accustomed to dealing with. With security intelligence, we were somewhat out of our league.

The police live in a world of criminal charges and convictions, testimonies and affidavits. There's never going to be a paper trail doing spook work. Of course, the CIA will have internal paperwork, but their reports never make it out of Langley's control. The CIA, like CSIS, deals exclusively in security intelligence. We can never ever use their information on any legal proceeding, much less a sworn affidavit. The CIA doesn't have any legal authority inside the US. Their agents are not sworn law enforcement officers. In fact, they don't have any authority anywhere in the world. So we can never use security intelligence like we do criminal intelligence from other US law enforcement agencies. US One only provides us intelligence so that, at a tactical level, we don't walk into a proverbial ambush. No memos, no paper of any kind. A secured call is rare. Information is passed only in personal conversation. Plausible deniability is the order of the day. But there is good reason intelligence is done this way. Canadian court disclosure rules require the police to disclose virtually every relevant thing to the defense. Information lent by our intelligence partners have caveats attached to them, for intelligence purposes only. That means it cannot be actioned. The intelligence shall not be shared with third parties without the originator's permission. Hence the information isn't technically in our possession. And if the intelligence was never ours, then we have no control over it. Neither in our possession nor having control of it, we do not have the legal obligation to disclose it. This is one of the many rules of cloak-and-dagger—essentially, you know that I know that you know that I know … but, really, you don't know until I let you know. It goes on forever.

The US One information was conflicting. But Jabril's information seemed to corroborate what was obviously the most plausible version. Nasser Tushanni, the son of an Afghan drug lord, was the only common telephone contact on the Baloch brothers' phones. Both Adham and Armaan were the targets of our investigation because a confidential informant reported that they moved chemical precursors for a MEOC group. The Baloch were predominantly Sunni Muslims, while the MEOC group was predominantly Persian, Shi'ite. From

what we knew of these sects, they were not in bed together on criminal enterprises. What we did know was that, recently, the Hazaras, a
Shi'ite community residing in the ghettos of Quetta, had been the
target of ethnic cleansing by Sunni extremists who espouse al-Qaeda
ideology. On the other side of the extremism coin were the Shi'ite of
Hezbollah. Although Lebanese in origin, they were supported by the
Iranian theocracy. The "Party of God" extoled religious revolution
and the propagation of the Shia faith. In the world of terrorism prac-
titioners, Iranian and Lebanese factions of Hezbollah were referred to
as just Hezbollah, one and the same. Judging by who they associated
with, my best guess was that the Baloch brothers were Sunni. I supposed there was an easy way to find out: Just ask the family.

I contacted our International Operations branch about getting
our liaison officer in Islamabad to conduct inquiries in Quetta about
the Baloch brothers. There was also the matter of the NOK to deal
with. Adham's immediate family was his wife and two young children. *We should attempt to notify the wife*, I thought. I ended up speaking with our liaison officer to Islamabad. He said he would gladly
do the NOK, but he suggested that I really think about whether I
wanted to conduct inquiries in Quetta.

"Pakistan is a third world—er—*developing* nation," he said. "There's
no way to predict what the local authorities will do to the family
members. The wife may be subject to threats or, worse, extortion,
particularly when they find out about the money."

I said that the nature of our investigation might not necessitate
the inquiry, since it looked like the matter would just be passed on to
a drug unit anyway. So I asked the LO to facilitate contact with the
family for NOK purposes only. Besides, I had a pile of exhibits seized
from the apartment with no one to return them to. If the wife would
come to Canada or authorize someone to take the exhibits back on
her behalf, I could wash my hands of them. The important bits had
already been forensically replicated anyway. We took human rights
issues very seriously, even abroad. We needed to weigh the benefit the

information would provide our investigation against the risk of harm to witnesses, or, in this case, the family.

I received a text from Connie Weathers to meet her for coffee downstairs. I grabbed Ameena from her desk and we headed down together.

"Where do I start? This is kind of messy," Connie opened. She explained that in 2006, Pakistan and the UK designated the Balochistan Liberation Army (BLA) as a terrorist entity. It was believed that the BLA today was based inside Afghanistan and was financially supported by the Indian government. They attacked Pakistani Forces, hence the terrorist designation. This would have been a simple story of the Baloch waging war against Pakistan for independence and self-determination, but there were also allegations of ethnic cleansing of non-Baloch minorities in Baloch territory. During the Afghan war, it was the Soviets who supported the BLA. Back in 1973, Pakistani police located caches of weapons inside the Iraqi embassy in Islamabad. The weapons were in boxes labelled with diplomatic exemption markings. These caches were reportedly bound for Baloch rebels. So the alignments were US, India, and Iraq on the one side, and then the Soviets, Afghanistan, and Pakistan on the other. They were each trying to destabilize the other, as well as their respective alliances.

"Are criminal entities here in Canada financing the BLA? I don't know. I did ask our MIO in the region to report on the latest intel analysis on the BLA," Connie continued. "I'm sure you already know; the US finally designated the BLA earlier this year. That's suspiciously recent, if you ask me."

The CBSA deployed Migration Integrity Officers, or MIOs, alongside RCMP and CSIS liaison officers at strategic Canadian embassy locations worldwide. The MIO was their first line of intelligence, collecting information on high-risk individuals traveling to Canada. MIOs had access to visa databases and could rescind visas issued under fraudulent circumstances. MIOs could stop people from boarding aircrafts bound for Canada. They also gathered, analyzed, and reported on intelligence related to irregular immigration and national security matters. "Irregular migration" is the polite nomenclature for the refugee or asylum-seeking process. Regular immigration channels are the more common family sponsorship or business categories.

Back in 2016, during the European refugee crisis, it had been Connie who had delivered the ministerial briefing that helped the Canadian government decide, given the number of refugees seeking entry, how many to admit into the country. Connie pointed out that the images the world saw on television—those of immigrants desperately flocking to the borders and refugee camps—were not wartime refugees. There were pressures to address the safety of families in war-torn Syria. That was the priority of the Canadian government. Syria had become a battleground for likely the most chaotic conflict in history. There were multiple warring parties and ever-shifting alliances and splintering: It was ISIL versus the Free Syrian Army (FSA); versus Jabhat al-Nusra (JN); versus YPG Peshmerga; versus Russia, Iran's Quds Force (IRGC-QF), and Bashar al Assad's Syrian Army. It was the quintessential dog's breakfast. And the reasonable assumption anyone could make was that the UNHCR offices were jammed with Syrian refugees awaiting relocation to a safe country—but this was not the case. The greater numbers of refugees were actually Albanian economic migrants, who were not in imminent danger.

Connie advised the Prime Minister that CBSA needed to expedite the admission of Syrians but that the expedition should not be at the expense of diligent screening. "We risk letting the terrorist themselves into the country," she cautioned. Connie also advised the Minster that the screening process should be completed *in-region* because it would be too difficult to order the deportation of failed applicants who were already in Canada. So she put her money where her mouth was and assembled her own screening team and headed out to the region. Connie pulled rabbits out of hats when it mattered the most. Wanting to put its best foot forward, CBSA sent Connie to the front-line UNHCR staging points. She set up screening stations in two undisclosed locations in the Middle East. And when she got back, she hit the ground running. Connie never missed a beat.

This time around though, regarding our Baloch boys, I had been hoping to get more from her. "That's not a lot of info," I said to Connie.

"It's still worth a lunch, though," she said firmly. Like I said, there would be no bullying when it came to our Connie.

"Okay. My choice then. Thai. And you're driving," I said. I didn't ever mind chatting with her, especially not over lunch. Connie was so well-travelled and well-versed in intelligence analysis that I felt like I was attending a professional development course, only far more interesting.

FIRST DECEIT

The following week, the LO Islamabad sent me a secure message that Adham Baloch's father-in-law, Muhammad Towfique, would be arriving in Vancouver to claim the belongings of Adham, on behalf of his wife. Under the circumstances, I was prepared to release Armaan Baloch's property to him as well. He was the only kin to show up, after all. I made sure the LO Islamabad passed on our current office address in Surrey, British Columbia.

A couple of days later, I received a call from the Commissionaire at the front desk saying that Muhammad Towfique had arrived. The Commissionaire clued in to the fact that Towfique had come pre-pared, even having the file number memorized. I took the elevator to the lobby and escorted Mr. Towfique to the basement exhibit-holding facility. He didn't say much, restricting himself to one-word answers mostly, and not volunteering any information beyond what I asked him directly. He was rather cold, but perhaps that was cultural, or maybe the 29-hour flight he had just stepped off of to get here had something to do with it. It occurred to me that he was the first live Baloch I had ever met. Or so I thought.

I handed Mr. Towfique four banker's boxes worth of personal belongings— clothing items, watches, wallets, rings, and necklaces. Last were the documents that Ameena examined from the apartment. The remaining belongings, the ones we did not seize, were still sealed in the apartment. Those could be disposed of at his discretion.

Mr. Towfique didn't ask me anything. Not even if there was any money or items of value to be collected.

I escorted Mr. Towfique back to the lobby area where he was met by an individual I assumed to be his local guide, who had driven him to our office. Mr. Towfique thanked me, loaded the banker's boxes into the trunk of the vehicle parked out front, and then pulled away with his driver.

A day or two later, I got another call from Sergeant Tibbs. I went to his office alone, as I couldn't find Ameena. As I closed his office door behind me, Ian told me that he had just had a weird conversation with US One.

"Two things," he said. "First is one of your guy's father-in-law."

"What about him?" I asked.

"Well, US One says that his name is not really Muhammad Towfique. It is Muhammad Choudhry. And US One says the dude is Pakistani ISI."

"Inter-Services Intelligence? *What the fuck?!* How the hell did they know? And how did they know he had been here to the office?" This information was extremely upsetting, not just because we'd obviously been had, but because I had no idea as to why.

"Well, you know them, they got spies everywhere. They won't say. Probably had a *sat* on him the moment he arrived," Ian said.

"No fucking way," I said, shaking my head in disbelief. "There's no way you can *keyhole* this guy out of YVR. They needed to have foot surveillance on him. What's the other bad news?" I asked, bracing myself.

"Well, I asked US One if they would verify the Tushanni information. They're sticking to their official story. They've never heard of this Tushanni before," he said.

"Wait, you told me they said that Tushanni worked for them, and that he was treacherous," I said, my shock starting to curdle into anger.

"Yes, that's what we got at first, and unofficially. And I've never known them to go back on their word," Ian said.

"Hang on, did you mention the conflicting information?" I asked.

"Yeah, of course. He just said that the first guy I spoke to, my guy Mike, must've made a mistake," Ian said.

"So they have no record of Tushanni at all?" I was still in disbelief. Ian just shook his head.

I asked Ian if Ameena had spoken to him about the information she got from her contact Jabril Yusufzai. He said that he'd seen her at coffee the other day and they'd discussed it.

"I don't get this," I said. "Nasser Tushanni is an Afghan warlord's *son*. Don't tell me the CIA doesn't have a jacket on him. Something stinks here," I insisted. When dealing with the CIA, there's always a game afoot. I definitely wasn't feeling the trust on this particular file.

"What about the Sisters?" I pushed on. By "Sisters" I was referring to our favourite neighbourhood spooks, CSIS. The Service, also known in the industry as the Sisters, are the other half of Team Canada in the national security game.

"Nothing," Ian said.

"Was that a full de-con?" I asked.

"Yeah, nothing. Not even on their radar," he said.

Good, I thought. *That means Tushanni is fair game.* That was what de-con was really good for, after all: to ensure that we didn't fly into their traps and they didn't trip into ours. *Okay, so Tushanni doesn't work for them—that means he is for real.*

I marched back to my desk and contacted Connie to facilitate a CBSA lookout for Tushanni. Canada doesn't gate-keep outbound or departing travellers at the airports. Unlike most countries that stamp passports both inbound and outbound, Canada has not made it a practice to track people leaving the country. This often poses difficulty for police and immigration officers. The police waste their time looking for people who have left the country months or even years ago. The lookout is only for inbound travellers.

I needed some intelligence on Tushanni. I needed to work in concert with CBSA and develop their independent grounds to conduct a secondary inspection and interview the next time he returned from abroad. My NS unit needed to talk to their NS unit. The easy way was for me to dump the intel on Connie, and it would work its way to the border inspectors. One exception in this case, though: I needed to specifically instruct her not to share the info with DHS across the border. I wanted US One to think their ploy had succeeded.

In the meantime, Ameena was already speaking to FINTRAC to get financial intelligence on Tushanni. When I started in national security, I was under some delusion as to what capabilities FIUs had. I assumed that Canada's banking system would all be integrated into a singular network. That means that all the reporting could be done automatically. I expected that all the data would be amalgamated into a collective where algorithms could be run through the data. This would be the optimal way to identify high risk accounts and transactions. A risk-based approach would allow compliance personnel to selectively dive more granularly into suspicious account behaviour. And banks could then share intelligence through the same portals. Sure, there would be privacy issues that needed to be addressed and overcome but providing the shared account information was represented only as numbers, then privacy could be maintained. The tombstone data, like account holder names, addresses, and contact numbers, would be excluded from the dataset. Hence, in my sci-fi mind's eye, Big Brother would only be profiling accounts and analyzing account behaviour. If the police wanted the identity of the account holder of a high-risk account, then they could go before a judge and obtain a search warrant or a production order. That was my pipe dream. I thought that financial people much smarter than me had worked this through.

But I soon learned that reality was very different. I learned from the bankers that almost every financial institution operated such different systems that integration to the level I imagined was never even considered. There was no will in the industry to do it, and no political will from government to drive it—in fact, I doubt anyone's even suggested it. Financial institutions are run by institutionalized think. They think inside the box. Furthermore, every financial institution's legal branch has a different threshold for privacy, and they can't even agree on legal definitions. So in reality, banks only do barebones compliance. They don't protect anyone; they just pay lip service to mandatory compliance regimes. There is zero sincerity there. And you wonder why money laundering is so prevalent.

The Financial Action Task Force (FATF) is not a sanctioning organization. They couldn't stop a little girl from sucking her thumb. Then, you ask, what do FINTRAC and the FIUs actually record? The short answer is $10,000 and over, anything suspicious, such as people depositing smelly money, and cross-border remittances. This poses several problems. The sheer size of the data, absent of any context, is just that: reams and reams of useless numbers. Moreover, ten thousand dollars today is not a large sum of money, so there are a bazillion meaningless reports. Suspicious or unusual transactions need a person involved the transaction to report its suspicious nature. So, you can imagine that there is no consistency as to what "suspicious" or "unusual" might mean from one person to another. The reporting of those is never consistent and is prone to false positives or non-reports. And here's the clincher: Of the millions of transactions that occur daily, how many still involve people? Computers are smarter nowadays, but they have yet to develop the capacity to report a suspicious occurrence based on human behaviour.

Nasser Tushanni had travelled to Afghanistan 17 times in the past year. I expected that he would be re-entering Canada soon. It was not illegal to bring cash into Canada, but it was illegal not to declare amounts at or past the threshold of $10,000. Failing to declare the cash would result in a fine, forfeiture, or both, depending on the circumstances.

The authority that I had worked with over the years was the Proceeds of Crime Money Laundering and Terrorist Financing Act (PCMLTFA). It is the bible of what is today called Threat Finance, which is inclusive of criminal proceeds and terrorist resourcing. This is also the authority that empowers FINTRAC and mandates the reporting of threshold, suspicious, and cross-border transactions.

The FINTRAC analyst mentioned that Tushanni had been declaring hundreds of thousands in US cash every other time he returned to Canada. He declared the origin of the money as the sale of family property in Afghanistan. These declarations are just that—they are not necessarily confirmed with documentation at the point of entry. And even if the documents are examined, there is still no process to verify the authenticity of the document. The Act clearly defines what needs to be declared. And everyone understands what cash is. But there is no clear definition of what "monetary instrument" means in the Act. Stored value cards like prepaid credit cards can store very large values in small stacks of cards. Yet nobody ever checks for these cards. There are no instruments to actually read the value of these cards at any point of entry. Canada gets an E- for effort here. But we're in good company. I don't know of any country that tracks these either. And according to my member of parliament, neither the previous nor current government wants to do anything about it. You are welcome to guess why.

Ameena wanted to interview Nasser Tushanni. He had never been subjected to a secondary examination at a point of entry before, so there was no historical information on him. But his newly discovered association with organized crime and methamphetamine trafficking changed things now. His connection to the Baloch brothers now gave law enforcement the grounds to conduct an interview and scrutinize his funds. All of a sudden, he'd be showing up on our radar. I was certain this wasn't something he would have anticipated.

⊕ ⊕ ⊕

Several weeks later, I received a voice message form the Passenger Assessment Unit (PAU) of CBSA. PAU screens through flight manifests of inbound commercial aircraft. This is made possible by an agreement between border services and commercial air carriers operating in Canada. The PAU officer calling was responding to my lookout request. Tushanni was booked on Lufthansa LH492, arriving from Frankfurt that afternoon. Sometimes there's not a lot of advanced notice for these things. At times, the warning arrives when the subject is already aboard an inbound aircraft. It was a good thing that the flight from Frankfurt was long enough to give us a buffer. There is much that goes into orchestrating a proper interview.

"Ameena," I said over the phone. "Your guy is arriving on a Lufthansa flight from Frankfurt. ETA is 14:25."

"Okay," she replied. "Call CBSA and set up an interview room. I'll give the CSIS duty officer a courtesy call."

I already mentioned orchestration of interviews. Well, on security matters, we coordinate with CSIS and CBSA. CSIS will conduct their interview first, if required. CSIS is not a law enforcement agency. They do not possess police powers. So their presence does not present jeopardy to the suspects. They can just proceed to the interview. If the police speak to the suspects first, they will invoke the Charter of Rights and Freedoms, which means that the suspects have to be read their rights and be provided access to a lawyer. Once these rights are invoked, they cannot be withdrawn. It would be like putting the proverbial genie back in the bottle. We need to respect our place in line.

"CSIS has no interest in talking to Tushanni at this time. But they want to sit in on the interview if they can. Do you have any concerns about that?" asked Ameena.

"That's fine with me," I replied. Unlike what is often portrayed on hyped-up cop shows on television, police agencies don't quarrel over jurisdiction. In reality, law enforcement agencies are very civil and professional towards each other. We're a family. Yes, we have quibbles, but they are mostly constructive. And, more often than not, it's a relief to hand the reigns over to another agency—all too often, just like us, partner agencies are overworked and understaffed. That being said, though, despite meagre resources and overwhelming workloads, law enforcement agencies always offer each other assistance whenever it's needed.

We had to get a move on to the airport. CBSA had agreed to conduct the secondary inspection but would get first dibs on evidence that was within their scope of enforcement. This was not only sportingly fair but also best practice.

When Ameena and I arrived, we were set up in the interview room just behind the secondary inspection line-up. We watched behind one-way glass as Tushanni was directed by the greeting (primary) officer to the secondary inspection line. The border officer took notes of his declarations and examined the contents of his luggage. After the secondary inspection, the CBSA officer escorted Tushanni into the interview room.

"At this point, the RCMP would like to speak to you," he said. "This terminates your interaction with the CBSA. We have no further authority to detain you." The officer noted the time in his notebook.

Earlier, Ameena had moved the furniture in the interview room. She had shoved the table against the corner wall and positioned the chairs around the two protruding sides of the table. This prevented the furniture from acting as a psychological barrier between the interviewee and the police interviewers.

"*Asalaam alaikum,*" Ameena greeted in Arabic. Peace be with you, a greeting among Muslims. I had forgotten that Ameena, although not a practicing Muslim, was schooled in Islam. In her youth, she had spent several weeks in a madrassa in Saudi Arabia, learning the Quran.

I wasn't sure how Ameena was going to conduct herself as the lead interviewer. Some traditional Muslims refuse to engage a female in lead, or even secondary, interviewer roles. All we knew about Tushanni was that he had first arrived in Canada as an LI, a landed immigrant, in 1976. His port of entry was Pearson International in Toronto. He became a citizen in 1980 and had been living in Vancouver since 1995. He had never had any contact with police. He'd had a British Columbia driver's license since 1996, one vehicle registered under his name, and not had so much as a traffic ticket in his name. Provincial records showed no ownership of any properties, and there were no records of his name in any corporate registrations. His only entry on the Police Records Information Management System (PRIME) was when he reported his Canadian passport lost or stolen in 2002. It was an administrative file; no police attendance was required.

"*Wa-Alaikum Salaam*," Tushanni responded. And unto you, peace. I'd always thought this call and response was one of the more beautiful things about the Muslim culture. It sure beats out "Good afternoon" which, in comparison, feels generic, impersonal, and distant.

We had already noted how well Tushanni spoke English while he was dealing with the CBSA officer on the other side of the one-way glass. Tushanni was quite fluent, even eloquent, in his mastery of English, betraying his higher Western education. I suppose being the son of a drug baron had its privileges. And, if I were a betting man, I'd wager that Tushanni, in addition to English and Pashto, also spoke Urdu, and possibly even Dari, which is the Persian dialect more closely related to Balochi.

So Ameena didn't bother with the next standard question: whether Tushanni required a translator.

Twenty minutes into the interview, Ameena realized that she was interviewing someone who knew the game, and who likely had a tremendous amount of experience making deals with Western authorities. Tushanni gave up nothing. He had a story for everything, and a reason for every aspect of his life that Ameena asked about. Tushanni said that his mother was Masub's third and least favoured wife. And as a result of that, he was not as economically advantaged as most people thought. He had worked the streets of Kandahar in early life (I thought it strange, though, that Tushanni was at retirement age now, and yet he possessed nothing on paper, or at least not here in Canada). He had a well-worn cover story. We got a sense that Nasser was long in the tooth with tradecraft, and he had us on our heels. We didn't have his pedigree. But Ameena wasn't giving up. She wanted something out of Tushanni, and she was going to get it. She actually looked like she was enjoying the interview. You see, one of the greatest perils of interviewing is giving up more than you learn, and skilled operatives live and die by this game. Ameena could see that Tushanni believed us to be inexperienced players, far below his caliber. But she also recognized a large ego when she saw one. Perhaps she would exploit his nurturing side. If she could keep him feeling like Shaq playing pickup basketball with a bunch of kids in an East LA playground, she could get Tushanni talking, or, at the very least, she could establish a rapport with him and set the stage for future contacts. It wasn't likely that we would recruit Tushanni as an informant—he was too wily for that—but maybe we could learn something he wasn't intending to teach us.

Ameena was a brilliant interviewer. I think her exposure to so many different cultures had left her with a unique depth of understanding. It provided her with multiple lenses through which to examine, interpret, and comprehend abstractive concepts. She saw the world in three dimensions. It's like the ability to put oneself in another's shoes and see things from behind their eyes. It is an incredible asset.

Tushanni began describing his childhood, how he had grown up playing football in city parks in Kandahar. He was improvising now, sharing nostalgias that were completely unrelated to the topic of the Baloch brothers. He had time to burn, so why not entertain the troops? He recounted how he had started working odd jobs for an American NGO operating in Northern Pakistan when he was in his early 20's, mostly "tour guiding" and "fixing" for the company employees who needed to traverse large expanses of country. His employment had him travelling extensively around the neighbouring regions, into Uzbekistan, Tajikistan, Kyrgyzstan, Turkmenistan, Kazakhstan, and even west of the Caspian Sea to Azerbaijan and Dagestan. But, as it was so long ago, he couldn't recall the exact name of the NGO—Pegasus something-or-other. It studied mineral resources and geological engineering. He said it was like being a local consultant to a large multinational. But he was never an employee of the firm, just a contractor, so he really didn't know the inner workings of the company.

Whatever Tushanni was selling, I wasn't buying. But Ameena kept going. She wasn't even really interviewing him anymore; Tushanni had taken the lead. He had now become the entertainer, like a stand-up comedian performing a monologue. So we just sat back, took a modicum of notes (or pretended to, anyway), and let the DV recorder drain its batteries.

Tushanni went on to give an account of a transport and logistics company he had once operated. Foreign companies with business interests in the region contracted his services, moving goods through the area. He even bussed people from the World Health Organization after the fall of the Soviet Union. He only bought land with his earnings. It was something that he learned from his father, Masub. He believed that arable land would be the last thing of value on earth after man degraded the planet. I thought that was a pretty apocalyptic outlook. But in a society steeped in the agrarian era, land is the only thing of value.

My mind began to drift. I started thinking about my last visit to Vietnam. I remembered going to the War Remnants Museum in Ho Chi Minh City. The museum staff reminded tourists that they would only be presenting the communist version of the story and recommended that visitors cross the street to hear the other, Western side. It then became clear to me that the Vietnam War was never about political ideology. In fact, politics was the furthest thing from the minds of farmers from either side, whose daily concerns were the weather and crop yields. The farmers who fought with the Viet Cong did so for the land their families had owned for millennia. Land was the only thing they possessed. In tribal regions, land is still the most desirable thing, because one can use it to produce food. So when they were told that the bogeyman was coming, and that they would lose their land, as some South Vietnamese already had through corruption and land-grabbing practices, they fought for the only thing of value in their lives. They knew that if they lost the land, they may as well just kill themselves. There would be nothing left for the next generation, certainly not their family's dignity. So they fought. And they fought with such ferocity that superior technology, armament, and tactics could not defeat.

I forced myself to tune back into Tushanni's tireless narrative. Now he was talking about how he had liquidated his properties in Afghanistan and moved his money to Canada. He claimed that, since arriving to Canada in 1976, he had been working in an import/export business. He said that after he earned Canadian citizenship, he started spending more time in Kandahar. He never registered a company before because he worked mostly as a middleman. He said he traded in textiles and preserved foods, but that he now only does deals sporadically. His aim was to slow down as he headed into retirement.

With a few insistent course corrections from Ameena, he casually conceded that he'd first met Adham when a mutual friend had asked him to help settle the Baloch brothers in Vancouver. Then Ameena hit the target directly. "What's been your connection to the Baloch brothers since?"

"There are a couple of reasons I keep in touch with them," he replied, without batting an eye. "First, they are friends. I see them socially in the community. And I travel to Afghanistan and Pakistan all the time, looking for business. I specialize in importing seasonal items, so I need to keep ahead of my supply chain. They wanted to send money, foodstuff, or small items back home all the time, so I took things back for them."

"What kind of items?" Ameena asked.

"Anything," he replied. "Last month, Adham wanted me to carry a box of Samsung phone covers for his wife. I think she owns a stall in a market there."

Two hours of chatting with Tushanni, though entertaining, seemed like a waste of time. Worse, it was a dead end for our investigation. At least I was confident that he hadn't learned anything from us, other than the fact that we were conducting a drug investigation. And he might have been skilled enough to suspect that we were with National Security.

After we released Tushanni, Ameena was quiet, immersed in deep thought.

"The name of the NGO," I said as Ameena pulled out of the airport parkade.

"Yeah, Pegasus," she replied. "I wonder what he did for the CIA. He did say what regions he had been in. I wonder if we can confirm those with assets in the theatre. The problem now is, the CIA was usually our first stop for foreign intel. I think we need to bypass them for now. I've got some ideas."

"Jabril?" I asked.

"Yep," she said. "I think we need to up the game here. We need someone on the ground in the region. There's no way we'd be allowed to fly to Kandahar for this file. Not yet, anyway."

I feared what Ameena was thinking. She was not one to stick to the books. She had a few sayings pinned to the divider on her desk. One of them was, *Rules: a guide for the wise, a bible for fools.*

I had a nagging suspicion that, despite what Tushanni had said, the NGO Pegasus was directly related to Tushanni's relationship with the CIA. One need not import too much imagination here. Historically, that's how the CIA operated. The leaked Panama Papers alleged that

the CIA straw accounts that were held at Mossack Fonseca were utilized to move money to other NGOs. That was also the methodology
utilized in the Iran-Contra affair. The CIA used front companies and
NGOs with layered ownerships to distribute off-the-books money.
This is not the same as the US government using covert accounts for
sensitive expenditures. These funds often originate from outside the
US and are not acquired from the tax base.

We drove back to division headquarters. *This is going to be a dead-
end file*, I fretted. Ameena was lost in her own thoughts. You couldn't
tell by the meticulous way she drove, but there was definitely something eating at her. I think that she knew that there was more meat
to this bone, but the question was how to get at it, and where to start.
Ameena was a bloodhound when she caught a whiff of something.
She had this dogged determination to finish what she started. And
I could tell from the distracted look in her eye right now that this
investigation would be no different. She would allow no stone to be
left unturned.

The police are attentive to neither the politics nor the sociology of
terrorism. The police are creatures of templates and processes. Was
the act committed? Was there the intent to commit the act? Was
the act proscribed by law? And boom, there you have it: Proceed
with the prosecution. It is a purely reactive organizational culture.
Before Ameena showed up, the unit's understanding of terrorism was
a roughly hewn patchwork of misconceptions lifted straight out of
prime-time television. Ameena was incensed by that when she first
joined the force. She couldn't believe the incompetence of senior
management. I remember her saying, "It's a good thing the terrorists
don't really hate us Canadians. I wouldn't sleep at night knowing
we're the only ones between them and the public we're supposed
to protect."

Ameena intuitively understood that there was something bigger at play. She knew to differentiate terrorism from criminality. And she understood the power of ideology. She had sacrificed several promotional opportunities to move up the ranks to earn her expertise in terrorism and had subsequently lectured on terrorist resourcing at the post-graduate level in a local university. She facilitated the terrorist financing course for the Federal Training Branch for as long as I can remember (she may still look like one, but she was no spring chicken). She was hosted by the US Department of Defense for her fellowship at the George C. Marshall European Centre of Security Studies in Germany, and was widely considered to be the most knowledgeable threat finance technician in the country.

The irony was, the RCMP didn't even know she was in the inventory. While terrorism experts around the globe consulted with her on matters of financial typologies and methodologies, our dumb ass senior management teams were completely oblivious to her abilities. In fact, some were leery of her capabilities.

Within the organization, Ameena needed to keep explaining the differences between anti-terrorism and counterterrorism. There were some people managing NS units across the country that, erroneously, still used the terms interchangeably. "Newsflash!" Ameena would yell. "We do not, as a rule, do counterterrorism in Canada! Proactive, kinetic strategies that characterize the academic definition of counterterrorism are in contravention of due process of law and the Canadian Charter of Rights." Counterterrorism is what JTF2 and Canadian Forces do on foreign soil.

Police Emergency Response Teams (ERTs) are our equivalent of the all-purpose tool. ERTs are utilized to mitigate risk during critical situations. But not even ERTs conduct counterterrorism in Canada, not by any stretch of the imagination. They may end up shooting the odd terrorist (which happened recently in Ontario), but that work is chalked up to critical response, not counterterrorism.

Having arrived back to the office, we headed to our project room to meet with the team. On the way, we were told to gift wrap the file and hand it over to the drug unit. But it's hard to let down something before you've figured out what it is. We knew we were missing the big picture somewhere. And there was something very unsettling about Nasser Tushanni. I just couldn't quite put a finger on it.

At the meeting, I said, "So let's recount. We have two dead brothers, immigrants from Balochistan."

"I don't know about you, but it seems to me that they died to protect something," said Ian Tibbs.

Then Renner piped up. "No one has ever killed themselves to avoid a drug charge, in B.C. of all places. They would've gotten—what? Having had no criminal record, nothing more than a suspended sentence? Probation?"

"Protecting someone else?" I guessed.

"And not so much as an Allahu Akbar before they jumped," Renner threw in.

"We are missing something. This is not a drug file," said Ameena. "Tushanni is just too greasy. We need to dig deeper into their connections. If this were a homicide, we would be looking into the drug associates. Somehow, because they died, we have no one to investigate on the terrorism nexus. And drug section will be taking the trafficking investigation, which will likely wrap up pretty quickly. I guess we're out of the game." Ameena added, "The answer here is likely to be found in Pakistan or Afghanistan. We need an economic workup of the Baloch brothers."

"How do you suppose they were sending the $31,000 in traveller's cheques? And by whom? Tushanni?" I said. "Who the hell uses traveller's cheques anymore anyway? Are those even real? We need to send them down to the lab for counterfeit analysis."

"This is like playing lawn chess from inside a trench. We can't see where our pieces are," Ameena said. "We only know that there's a larger game at play here. These guys were working with the North Shore MEOC group. What's up with that?"

Ameena had been saying for years that the Iranian group on the North Shore was actually Hezbollah, and that the group had begun settling in amidst the Iranian diaspora around 1987 when Citizenship & Immigrations Canada was struggling to deal with a spike of refugee applicants. Lebanese proponents of either organization would land in Canada without the proper visas and request asylum. The asylum seekers would openly declare that they were members of Hamas or Hezbollah and were seeking refuge from the intifada. And Canada then flung its doors open and welcomed them with open arms. Of course, the diaspora continued to grow, and Hezbollah criminal activities began to dominate north of the Burrard Inlet, completely unchecked, and with absolute impunity. From there, the IRGC-QF joined the fray and established what Ameena labeled a "cloud economy," an economic network of hub-and-spoke corporate shells with multiple bank accounts, whose sole purpose was to protract Iranian proliferation activity to circumvent the global embargos against it. Ameena aptly called it a cloud because the entities rarely conducted legitimate economic activities with non-Persian Canadian businesses.

It was important for analysts to understand Iran itself. Iran had been under an economic embargo since the 1979 hostage-taking situation at the US embassy in Teheran. Today's Ayatollah is Ali Khamenei, the supreme leader of the theocracy. Iran's president, currently Hassan Rouhani, only has guardianship of Iran's domestic affairs; it's the Ayatollah Khamenei who controls all international activities. The Iranian Revolutionary Guards Corp. (IRGC) is the elite military force charged with the safeguarding of the Islamic (Shi'ite) regime from both foreign and domestic threats. And the Quds Force (IRGC-QF) is the cream of the IRGC. The QF is charged with unconventional warfare, foreign intelligence, and extra-territorial operations. Today, the IRGC-QF is fighting in Syria in support of Iran's long-time ally Bashar al-Assad.

Since the founding of Hezbollah (Party of God) in Lebanon in the early 80's, its been financially backed by Iran. Henceforth, the West termed its operations as "state sponsored terrorism." Intrinsically, Hezbollah maintains an arm in Iran, both it and the QF are controlled by the Ayatollah. The US recalibrated the sanctions in 1987 for Iran's actions against shipping vessels in the Persian Gulf. The sanctions were expanded again in 1995 to include companies dealing with the Iranian government. The IRGC-QF was charged with developing strategies to circumvent the trade embargo against Iran. And sound analytical theory places the IRGC-QF as the orchestrators of the subjugation of Venezuela under Hugo Chavez. Venezuela became a de facto state of Iran, and a launch pad for all matters of economic trade and illicit activities. Iran did not just create a front company; they created a front *nation* to be its gateway to global trade.

In the region, Iran is the Dark Star. And the sphere of its influence is wide indeed. Correlative analysis puts Hezbollah squarely in the middle of the drug trade in the tri-border region of Brazil, Argentina, and Paraguay. Ameena believed that Hezbollah's influence then flowed northward, melding with cartels in Colombia and Mexico. This is an example of what criminologists call the Convergence Theory, meaning the convergence of transnational organized crime with terrorists.

Ameena told me back in 2011 that the US Department of Homeland Security heard testimony before the subcommittee on Counterterrorism and Intelligence. The testimonies all pointed to Hezbollah being active in Latin America. The testimonies included an analysis of the far-reaching implications of its activities in the region. In short, this was confirmation of Ameena's Dark Star theory. As early as 2012, Ameena had been trying to advise RCMP management of this threat, but all of it had fallen on deaf ears. That is because the RCMP had no criminal intelligence (oxymoron intended) on Hezbollah, and it could not see any of its impact on the streets of Canada. Worse, CSIS was non-reactive to her analysis. Moreover, better organizations had likewise failed to collate the intelligence sensibly. Apparently, no one does game theory matrices on geo-politics and global affairs anymore, at least not at the law enforcement level. The RCMP failed to realize that the cartel-sourced drugs hitting Canadian streets were products of Colombian and Mexican cartels advancing the Hezbollah syllabus. Police agencies from San Diego, California, all the way to Blain, Washington, only saw the street gang distributors of the drugs. While it is easier to link the cartels to the source of the drugs, it required more resources to identify Hezbollah operating above the cartels.

The ultimate result was that everyone continued to underestimate Hezbollah's tenacity. Hezbollah is bigger, and more powerful, than any organized crime group. It has the capacity for unimaginable violence. Recall the twin suicide bombings against the multinational peacekeeping force in Beirut in 1983 that killed 307 people; the attack on the US barracks that day killed 241 American service personnel. Although some academics place this event before the creation of Hezbollah, there are no better suspects. In fact, this event could have been its inauguration. What bike gang, what mafia family, what cartel can hold a candle to Hezbollah?

In 2016, Ameena and I briefed the FBI in Oakland, California, on suspected activities of Iranian-backed organized crime in Vancouver. Ameena described the configurations of numbered companies and the operation of the cloud economy. She demonstrated how they held shell companies with local organized crime elements to invest criminal proceeds in the venture capital markets. The FBI was more concerned about the drug traffic up and down the I-5 corridor, from Mexico to Canada, and Ameena revealed to them that the corridor is a singular stream from Latin America, terminating in Alaska. I saw the FBI agents' incredulous reactions.

Then Ameena brought to their attention a Canadian who was serving time in San Quentin for violating the Special Economic Measures Act sanctions against Iran. "*This* is the face of Hezbollah in the West Coast." Presenting a PowerPoint slideshow of a company registration document which named the Canadian subject as its only director, Ameena handed the FBI the link between Hezbollah and pump-and-dumps in the venture markets. Then she handed them another nugget: She said that while HUMINT suggests that the individual is associated with Hezbollah, the typology of his corporate criminality is signature IRGC-QF. Ameena said that the easiest way to differentiate their activities is to bifurcate the methodology. Hezbollah is charged with criminal enterprise, while the QF activities are sterile, mostly business conduct for proliferation purposes.

When Ameena identified the subject and the company, and showed that the previous director of the company had been a gangland boss they all knew, all of a sudden the analysts in the back row frantically opened their laptops and began querying the case. Ameena aptly summarized, "You want proof of convergence theory? Here it is, in black and white. And this did not happen in LatAm, folks; it occurred a couple of blocks away." I looked around the room at the stunned crowd. Then I looked at Ameena. I heard my inner voice saying, "Ya go, girl! Make 'em stuff it up their pipes and smoke it."

Intelligence has a shelf life. Some agencies treat it as if it were a commodity that retains value. They gotta give their heads a shake. If you can't find a consumer for your intelligence, it is as useless as the proverbial balls on a priest. Yet nearly 20 years after 9-11, these intelligence-sharing meetings remain somewhere between a pissing contest and a waste of time. My team tries to bust through the silos and openly share intelligence at ground level, but we rarely get anything back. And we are in sore need of intelligence portals, think tanks for policy guidance. We need predictive analytics. We need to be better. Despite all this, what I'm afraid of is that, one day, we'll finally get up to the pinnacle of our craft and find nothing but a mirror. And in that mirror is the sole image of us staring back at ourselves. Yes, we were the cause of all that mess. There was never anybody else.

In the US are a number of think tanks like the Washington Institute for Near East Policy, the RAND Corporation, and my personal favourite, the DKI Asia Pacific Centre of Security Studies. That last one is located in Hawaii. Scientists substantiate facts while politicians bend them. I've spoken with researchers in these think tanks, and the common theme among them is that they would be happy if the government actually took their advice half of the time. That's some pretty sad wastage of brain power.

After the meeting, Ameena and I headed back to my desk and poured over a map of Balochistan. We had learned from the LO that Adham and Armaan Baloch were Hanafi Sunni Muslims. The MEOC group, Hezbollah, are Shi'ite. Hezbollah operatives are not exactly going to carry Hezbollah membership cards—it's not that kind of country club—so the only way to know who they are is through their objectives, how they operate, and the commitment level of each individual. These guys know our tradecraft better than we know them ourselves. They are more practiced, much hungrier, and never display the kind of complacency that we are guilty of. A member doesn't quit counter-surveillance ops because she has to pick up her son from soccer, or daughter from ballet class. We are outclassed at every turn with their level of investment in the game. I often tell the guys from the drug division, "You want to burn your investigation? Go do surveillance on them."

Before history messed with the natural tribal borders of Central Asia, people of Baloch ethnicity broadly occupied territory currently inside Afghanistan, Iran, and Pakistan—I pointed to these places on the map with my finger, although Ameena, looking at the map from over my shoulder, definitely already knew where these places were.

Shi'ite Muslims are a minority among the Baloch people, and we wondered aloud whether there was any strategic significance to the Baloch brothers working for Hezbollah. The Baloch reside in a distinct geographic area, and the politics in the region have given rise to a separatist movement. The Balochistan National Movement (BNM) used to be the more vocal of the nationalist organizations, and likely the best financed. There was an intelligence analysis written in 2003 that the BNM was going to splinter. And there was concern that the more militant faction, the one disposed to violence, would dominate the leadership. As it turned out, the rise of the BLA proved this analysis correct.

I contacted the Islamabad LO and asked if I could obtain banking information from Quetta, Karachi, and Peshawar. The LO asked me what exactly I was going to ask for. "The usual," I said, as in account opening documents, signature cards, credit card information, savings and chequing account transactions, safety deposit boxes, electronic fund transfers, etc. The LO said, "Look, let me ask the Americans. They're the only ones who can put that together. They likely have to buy that information for us. And, oh, you won't be able to use it as evidence. Intel only," he said.

"Damn," I muttered, "Then what's the point? 'K, copy that, disregard." I put the phone down, disappointed. But I should have thought it through first. With all our rules of evidence, there is no way we could have ever used that information. Our courts won't accept their affidavits, so unless we can fly witnesses back to Canada to testify, all that evidence would be hearsay in a court of law. Life gets confusing when you shuffle between security and criminal intelligence.

Ameena then got a call piped through from Jabril Yusufzai. He wanted to pass on information about Ameena's earlier inquiry concerning Mohammad Choudhry, a.k.a Towfique, the Pakistani ISI agent who had come to retrieve the personal belongings of the Baloch brothers. The ISI is an enigma in intelligence circles. It is an extremely capable agency structured in the image of British

Intelligence but is now far and away from its original Western roots and sympathies. Ameena suspected that the ISI was likely monitoring proponents of the BLA. And if the BLA is in Canada, then it certainly conducts financing here. How the hell could it not? Everybody and their dogs raise money here.

Choudhry's arrival confirmed to us that the ISI has been monitoring the BLA internationally. I thought it was rather reckless of him to risk coming here. Connie checked his travel history and confirmed that he had entered the country just the day before he had met with me. This was Choudhry's first travel to Canada. ISI isn't known to be reckless, so there must have been a bigger reason for Choudhry's recent activities. I recalled how it struck me as strange when Choudhry was collecting the brothers' belongings that he had not asked me about money. When families must deal with burial expenses and transportation, money is the first item in discussions. I had given him all the meager possessions that had been recovered from the apartment, minus the traveller's cheques. Given all the circumstances of this case and the preponderance of the evidence, including the manner in which the cheques were secreted, the balance of probabilities lean toward criminal gains.

I had to remind myself that this was cloak-and-dagger work. Might the Baloch brothers have been working for the ISI? Could Choudhry have been their handler? Because if that were true, then it was probable that the ISI was actually monitoring Hezbollah in Canada. They could have inserted the Baloch brothers into the MEOC group they were working. And if that were the case, then it begged the question: Could Hezbollah be supporting the BLA? Alliances are formed, severed, and reformed quickly in these groups. They are volatile, at best. One can't afford to miss a single intel report.

Ameena put Jabril's call onto the phone's speaker so that we could both hear what he had to say about Nasser Tushanni. He said that his contact was not an FBI source, rather he found him through his family's contacts in Afghanistan. Jabril was willing to give us the contact, but then wanted to wash his hands of it; it was important that his own agency not find out that he had passed this contact on to us, and he needed to be kept out of it for personal reasons. The contact had asked for a meeting, but Jabril had been advised that it needed to be a clandestine handoff—we would be on our own.

After hastily agreeing to Jabril's terms, he went on to admit, in an undertone, that the contact was actually a blood relative, Jabril's second uncle, who had fought with the *mujaheddin* during the Russian-Afghan war. His uncle owned the lowdown on Tushanni. Typically, Jabril would have asked us to fly to Kandahar to meet with his uncle, but the man had run afoul of certain Afghan Taliban chieftains some years ago and now resided in Waziristan, just over the Afghan border in the frontier region of northwest Pakistan. There, he was under the uneasy protection of the Tehrik-i-Taliban Pakistan, known as the TTP or the Pakistani Taliban (which ISI had helped to establish in the early seventies, with the help of American funding; the TTP was now a designated terrorist organization).

"So Jabril wants us to meet with the TTP?" I asked after Ameena had ended the phone call.

"Not those guys," Ameena said. "Just the one guy. The uncle."

But the caveat was that we would have to travel to the region by ourselves. Once there, we would need the assistance of our LO to Pakistan. He would ask the Pakistani authorities to guide us through.

But ... these guys are terrorists, I thought. There was no way we could get official assistance from the Pakistani government on this matter. Hell, we couldn't get official assistance from our own people. This was something that would need to be pulled off like black ops. Plus, there was a travel bulletin for Waziristan—as in, *don't fucking go there*.

Several years back, one of our unit members travelled to Waziristan to investigate the hostage-taking of Brenda Gadd, a Canadian from Burnaby, B.C. She was purportedly abducted by a Waziristan warlord along with two other aid workers. The warlord had allowed Gadd to call her former roommate to follow up with the ransom demands, so

I wrote a wiretap warrant to monitor Gadd's roommate's phone. The aid workers were released, unharmed, very early during the ordeal, but sadly, Gadd never made it out. She was in very poor health and the Pakistani authorities were adamant that the whole kidnapping was a ruse. The Pakistani police said she was a Muslim sympathizer and that she had been a willing participant in her own abduction, that the whole thing might have even been her idea. They went so far as to accuse her of sleeping with her captor, and because this was not her first visit to the area, the Pakistani police's position was that it was not her first rodeo, either. As one needed to have the protection of warlords to walk the streets unmolested in the frontier territories, I was highly skeptical of where the police were getting their information from, since they were obviously unwelcome in the area. But their story certainly provided them with a convenient out. A couple of years later, I heard that Gadd had passed away from her illness, dying in captivity, likely due to the lack of medical attention. I didn't care if she was a fraudster or some misguided little old lady; I just hoped that the label of Muslim sympathizer had no bearing on the Canadian government's decision to do nothing.

At the end of the day, Gadd was a Canadian. We had sat around a table with the International Operations team and ruled out an armed extraction option utilizing our JTF2. But I had seen the videos of Gadd pleading for the Canadian government to bail her out of her dilemma. The whole thing looked staged. Even the Taliban-like gunmen looked unconvincing. They stood flanking either side of Gadd who was sitting between them, the muzzles of their AK-47s trained at her. Although the videos did not show their faces, they did show their footwear. The Taliban were wearing brand new, sparkling white Nike runners. Not exactly combat gear for any place outside of a hardwood-floored basketball court.

So the Gadd investigation told us that we could at least operate in Waziristan. Our people had been there before. We still had our LO and the likely assistance of the Pakistani police. I liked adventures, but this was like no roadie we'd ever done. We were doing this trapeze act without a safety net. There was just the subtle matter of convincing our boss to let us go. We knew this was going to be a tough sell, but we could argue that the Baloch brothers were involved with an organization that threatens Canadian national security.

"You guys of course realize that even if you convince the Officer in Charge, all you'll have is his support to take this to National HQ. You will still need to convince the Commissioner to let you go. To make matters worse, there's a standing travel bulletin raised by foreign affairs for that area," warned Sergeant Tibbs.

Ameena and I had to present a solid argument for why we would need to go to Waziristan to advance an investigation on terrorist financing. "We could ride on the MEOC-Hezbollah connection, slap on the CSIS advisory that Tushanni was a T-financier and take it as far as we can," she argued. "It's game on. I'll prepare an Ops plan. Let's see if he'll sign it."

"Wait!" I barked. "What advisory? What T-finance?"

Just then, Staff Kenney called and asked us to both come to his office. We went in and grabbed a chair each.

"Close the door," Kenney said. "This is hot off the press. We got an advisory letter from CSIS after I told them about this Muhammad Towfique guy and what US One said about him."

The advisory letter from the spooks said that Tushanni had financed terrorist attacks in the past—I guess they'd found something in their holdings after all (I wondered if Jabril had looped intel up and over to the Service). The advisory did not specify where or when it had occurred; in fact, the advisory provided nothing specific. But it was all we needed. It brought back the terrorism nexus and that meant my unit was back in the game. The info didn't spell it all out, but the terrorist context put us back squarely on our national security mandate.

It is not unusual to receive single line intelligence debriefs from the FVEY. Chronological queues and context are scrubbed from the information so that it stands alone. Leaving anything else in may identify the source of the information, human or otherwise. The only thing needed was a corroboration of the information, and we were well under way. Looking for that corroboration may well have justified an extraterritorial investigation.

An advisory letter from CSIS was one that we acted on, because the information could be converted into criminal evidence; with HUMINT the informant agrees to testify in open court. A disclosure letter, on the other hand, was information we could not lawfully advance because it contained security intelligence that would not meet evidentiary standards. SIGINT were mostly intercepts that were acquired with Security Act warrants, not Criminal Code warrants.

The legal thresholds to acquire either are very different. Sometimes, intelligence comes from what we call the "high-side." By this, I mean information categorized above top secret. Some of us (not all) were indoctrinated to the special access level, which is the highest security clearance in the land. Need-to-know and right-to-know govern all security practices, no matter the clearance granted to an individual. This means that just because you have the clearance doesn't mean you can access everything. All intelligence is compartmentalized to keep control of exactly who knows the information. The Top Secret Special Access level (TS-SA) grants access to all human, signals, imagery, and measurements intelligence in the shared FVEY realm.

The CSIS advisory letter need not identify the source of information at the outset. But the information can be taken at face value, because later in court, CSIS will stand by their advisory. If it fails to do so, a prosecutorial recommendation will not be made, and charges will not be laid. If one had already been laid, it will be withdrawn by the prosecution services. Just like source debriefing reports, only the fact lines make it to distribution. The information had already been sterilized of anything that could identify the source. Some information may be too sensitive to disseminate. The mere fact that the information leaked out would already identify the source and place them in harm's way. There are measures for the special handling of sensitive material of this nature. There are occasions when CSIS goes before a judge alone to present secret information that will not be disclosed to the defense.

Ameena and I went to meet with our OIC, Superintendent Lorne Platts, the Deputy Criminal Operations Officer for Western Canada and the Yukon, a man of vast policing experience. They say that Lorne had forgotten more things about policing than most will ever learn. He was a man who, in his younger days, did no less than what *had* to be done. And he got the job done no matter the cost. The man worked like he owed the country a debt he could never repay, but he'd never count himself as a workaholic. Lorne was a man of superior standards and held everyone in the unit by them. He had a steel-cold calmness about him. He was an out-of-the-box thinker. And yes, the weak feared him. He was a tough boss. And you had to have your shit together by the time you walked into his office, as he did not suffer fools gladly. I'd worked for Lorne during my early days in uniform. I liked working for him because of his leadership. He stuck by his rules, and if you knew them, then your world was simple and predictable. Toughness aside, Lorne was very kind and he was considerate of people's time. He wasn't infallible, but he owned up to the unit's mistakes and redressed them—unlike the self-entitled new generation of management who don't know the definition of accountability.

"Abubakhar Mehdi," Ameena threw at Lorne. "That, sir, is the information I got out of an Afghan third party contact." Of course, she really meant her buddy Jabril. According to this TPC, Mehdi worked with Tushanni in the mid-70's. In our interview of Tushanni inbound at YVR, he told us he worked for an American NGO in Central Asia in the 70's. Finding out exactly what those guys were doing in the "Stans" in 70's could provide a clue as to what Tushanni's special skills were, and would likely give us an indication as to what he was up to today. We needed to analyze what was going on in the Stans back in those days. Importantly, we needed to research which NGOs were operating in the region before the collapse of the Soviet Union.

"What've the Soviets got to do with this timeline?" Lorne asked. Ameena just looked into his eyes for a second. "Oh, we're going back to that, are we? Okay..." Lorne sighed.

Ameena explained that, at that moment, US One wasn't playing ball with us. They had basically contradicted themselves on the Tushanni matter and we didn't exactly want to push any buttons they were sensitive about. The US is a long-time ally, so when their agencies are not playing nice in the sandbox, usually it's because we're standing on a nerve. I still didn't know how to treat their information on Muhammad Choudhry. Were they following him, or us?

"Look," said Lorne. "I want you to focus on the Tushanni T-financing vis-a-vis his associations with the Baloch brothers and likely Hezbollah as well. Don't stray from the script. We don't want to be extracting the two of you from frontier tribal areas. Up until last year, there were still TTP elements in the area. I can't see this evolving into a project file. But prove me wrong, please. At the very least, bring back some worthwhile intel to make your trip worthwhile."

"Yes, sir," Ameena said, beaming a smile. If anyone other than Ameena had proposed this mission, Lorne would have simply said, "Don't let the door hit you on the way out." *Prove me wrong*: That's Lorne's challenge to everyone. The odd thing was that he'd be happy if you did exactly that.

Foreign ops aren't like it is in the movies. We had to obtain country clearances from Pakistan through the LO. The country clearance advised the hosting government that we were bona fide law enforcement personnel seeking the assistance of their local police authorities to further our investigation in their land. We needed to carry our green diplomatic passports and use them to enter foreign countries. The last thing we needed was to be accused of spying. And no, we were neither authorized by our agency to carry our firearms into a foreign country nor were we granted that option by the country in question.

Now the academic question is: when there is no sovereign authority in the land we are about to enter, wouldn't it be prudent to bring along some protection?

SLUMMING IN ISLAMABAD

We met the LO Islamabad at the Marriott. Ameena wasn't very happy with our accommodations. There was an uneasy tension in this city. Maybe we were just new to it. Our hotel driveway and lobby were barricaded. So was the US embassy five miles away. Five thousand-pound concrete barricades were stacked in triple rows to prevent vehicle-borne IEDs. *These things won't protect us against car bombs,* I thought. They put them here to make us feel better, like hiding behind your popcorn box during a horror movie.

Ameena actually wanted to go dark for this meeting with Abubakhar Mehdi. We knew that US One knew we were here. We knew that the ISI knew we were here. Likely the QF knew we were here, too. There were a million people in this city, but it was a small village for the intelligence community. And one common mistake Westerners make is to seek Western comforts everywhere they go. The thing about our affinity for Western comforts is that the bad guys know exactly where to find us. That's why extremists bomb Western hotels and hangouts; that's where they find targets in high concentrations, some of high value.

Ameena said that we should have arrived under our undercover identities and stayed in a safe house. But she also knew that was CSIS's purview and not ours. We were supposed to stay in our lane. We did not have police powers in the region, and therefore we couldn't conduct investigations and gather evidence ourselves. Our own courts will not recognize extra-judicial evidence unless it is backed by a lawful authority in that region. So, we were purely on "observe and report" mode.

We needed to head out to Miranshah in Northern Waziristan. It was about 14 miles from the Afghan border. Ameena asked the LO Islamabad whether he had any fixers who could guide them to Miranshah. The LO said he would ask his local contacts but that it was near impossible to clean ourselves off. All the other intel units would know where we were headed.

"Fuck it," said Ameena. "You got any rupees?" she asked the LO.

"How much do you need?" he asked.

"This is my 084R expenditure voucher. Just front me as much cash as you can. I'll sign it over to you," Ameena replied.

That evening we snuck out of the service entrance utilized by Marriott hotel employees, and Ameena walked me out to the nearest night bazaar to get some local clothes. We conducted multiple heat checks to shed ourselves off any tails we'd acquired; we ended up crawling under the vendor tents several times, kind of like a human shell game but with two balls and many more cups. Then Ameena made me ditch my clothes in a manhole. At least I had been smart enough to pack my least favourite clothes for this trip. She made me buy Peshawari sandals despite thinking we would encounter rocky terrain.

"These look fucking ridiculous," I said.

"Go buy the modern version, you doofus!" she said endearingly.

She bought some head coverings for both of us, a veil for herself and a pakol hat for me. She also found an old, beat up bag. She looked like a local. A very pretty local. We did half an hour's worth of heat checks, in and out of restaurants, out through back doors, splitting up in market crowds, and doing some quick clothing changes as we went. Satisfied that we had finally lost our tails—we knew they were there—we went through the town in zig-zag fashion, through small streets and alleyways. She found a room to let and made me rent it out for the night. We looked like an ordinary travelling couple and the inn keeper could not be more disinterested (he was far more interested in the cricket match playing on his satellite box). So I grabbed the keys and walked up to the room.

We were exhausted from the trip. I couldn't remember when I'd last slept. That part I was used to, though. Every operation was different. Most of the time, we didn't leave the greater Vancouver area. But every now and then, we got thrown into situations where we had to improvise. Unlike every other aspect of policing, this one didn't really have an operational manual. It was like the Wild West of the 1800s. No laws—well, not really. It was also just outside ground zero to one of the most concentrated SIGINT and TK collection zones on the planet.

We had gone from -8 Zulu to +5 Zulu. That's a 13-hour time difference from Pacific Standard. I was so tired I couldn't even do the math to see what time it was at home. Normally, one would simply look at the network time on their cell phones, but we'd taken the batteries out of our phones when we left the Marriott. This was a frontier region we were headed to.

It is understood that the NSA monitors every cell phone in the region. They have voice identification systems that alert to captures of the comms of their targets. There will be armed drones, intel drones, AWACS, HASPs, and everything else flying overhead 24/7. But right then, there was only one kind of airborne object that had my attention: cockroaches. I fucking hate cockroaches, especially when they're in flight. Nothing is scarier than a flying cockroach. This is one phobia I will never get over. I'd rather face a knife wielding assailant in a dark alley than a flying cockroach while buck-naked in the shower. There in that flea-bitten rat's nest of a hotel with no hot water, there had to be a cockroach somewhere.

Ameena and I had to share the one bed. I was not about to sleep on the floor. The bed would be treacherous enough, with whatever microorganisms that may or may not have lived there. I slept with all my clothes on and wrapped myself up with the blanket head-to-toe. There was no way a cockroach was sneaking in under the blanket while I slept. This took priority over being in bed next to the most beautiful woman I knew. I only hoped my snoring didn't keep her awake.

After what felt like minutes after I had nodded off, Ameena nudged me awake. Six hours had passed and we needed to be out before daylight. I got up to take a pee and noticed that Ameena had already readied herself before waking me. I donned my local clothing and attached a fake beard to my chin (I couldn't grow a real one, so this would have to do). After Ameena re-adjusted it to my side burns (all the while chuckling), we headed out the door and scurried down the steps, past the night watchman manning the desk.

We had discussed this route even before we had left Vancouver. There is a depot nearby where people could board private transportation to various towns. This wasn't exactly a bus terminal; it was a corner of the marketplace that had been reserved for 6X6 trucks with canopied flat beds to pick up paying passengers. Some featured bench seats on either side of the floor, but most passengers had to sit on the floor. This explained to me why people carried what appeared to be step stools to sit on. It was the only buffer one had between his or her bottom and the hardwood truck bed. This was not going to be a comfortable ride.

We saw the Miranshah placard on one of the trucks and followed another couple climbing into the back. There was a conductor collecting fares, 450 rupees. At that price you just knew that this transport was not registered with any authority. On a proper bus, that was the price of the trip from Islamabad to Talagang, about a third of the distance. We were hoping that there were rest stops along the way because we hadn't packed any food. Plus, there were no toilets on the truck. I prayed that the ride was not too bumpy.

The trip to Miranshah took over six hours, traversing 220 miles of varied terrain. As it turned out, the roads were paved all throughout the journey. Incredibly, most of the travel time was attributed to navigating the Islamabad-Rawalpindi district where nearly everything you could think of was on the road. There were carts pulled by animals, auto-rickshaws or tuk tuks, overloaded motorcycles, taxis, trucks, and whatever else you could mount wheels to, including your mom's dressing table. Some trucks looked like buildings on wheels, with their colourful adornments in the unique local style. And the traffic jams were legendary. What was daunting was the number of vehicles on the road. But the drivers seemed to make efficient use of available space to create forward momentum. There were more lines of vehicles than there were lanes on the road.

The traffic may have been crazy, but at least the people didn't seem to be. For many in the West, their only impressions of Pakistan are based on media that paints it in a negative light. Pakistanis are a warm and welcoming people. There is a calmness about them that contradicts the tensions that surround their politics and religion. And Islamabad is a city of relatively modern design and engineering. It was only built in the 60's to replace Karachi as the modern capital. The streets were built using a modern grid layout, and apart from the traffic density, it is relatively easy to navigate.

Miranshah was where Brenda Gadd had met her end. And that's where we were heading now. Miranshah lies in a valley on the banks of the Tochi River, surrounded by the foothills of the Hindu Kush Mountains. Miranshah is the headquarters of North Waziristan, formerly known as a federally administered tribal region (FATA). In 2014, this was a battle corridor to oust the Taliban and other affiliated insurgent groups. Major General Zaffar Khan commented then that "North Waziristan was an epicentre of terrorism. Militants of all colour and creed were based here. The local population was made a hostage by them." It was the main base of the Pakistani Taliban. This is the area Bin Laden likely used to escape when the Americans sacked Tora Bora. And sentiments remained for the insurgents here. There was word that the Taliban were permitted to flee before the

Pakistani forces liberated this city. The same sentiments likely allowed Bin Laden safe passage through here. Just 70 or so miles to the north, as the crow flies, is the historic Khyber Pass, the gateway between Central and South Asia.

Aesthetically, Miranshah looked like a smaller Peshawar or Rawalpindi. The roads had the same content. Today, this area is open to tourism. Foodie groups had started to explore what gastronomical delights could be found there. We got off the truck at the Nizamia Mosque on the Bannu-Miranshah Road. Ameena was a homing pigeon on a mission. She knew exactly where to go. But of course, all this was foreign to both of us. What I found intimidating was the fact that we were off the grid. No one but us knew we were here. If I had fallen on my head and died, there would have been no one there to know who I was or where I was from. We were completely untethered.

I asked Ameena if we were in the right place and she said that her instructions from Jabril were clear. We were to get off at the mosque next to an Allah Noor petrol station that our truck would use to gas up. And from there, we were to cross the highway and deke into Idak Link Road, which wouldn't have a street sign (surprise, surprise) but was perpendicular to the highway, T-boning right at the mosque.

"K. Then what?"

"Oh, he'll find us," Ameena assured me.

The shadows were getting long. I hoped we had a place to bunk in for the night. But Ameena said that, for now, all I needed to know was that we would need to debrief Abubakhar Mehdi for several days. She said that Mehdi told her that he would tell us everything we needed to know. *Great*, I thought. *Because right now we don't know what it is we need to know.*

To kill time, Ameena began to tell me about her days back at the FBI Academy, and one particular night when she had gone out for drinks with Jabril at the Boardroom Quantico. Jabril had told her that the *real* story of 9-11 wasn't what was shared with the public.

And that conspiracy theorists had left an indelibly bad taste to alternate constructs about everything. Yet in Game Theory (the study of mathematical models of strategic interaction between rational elements), there was an even higher probability of an alternate narrative to 9-11. One chronological sequence that, above all others, is most mathematically probable.

"So, what has this hocus pocus got to do with our Baloch brothers and Tushanni?" I asked.

"Well," Amina continued, "everything has to do with relationships. Motive is born out of a need to satisfy characteristics of those relationships. I'm talking relationships of values here. Numbers."

"I'm lost," I conceded.

Ameena said, "Look. It really is just about cause and effect. You can accurately determine a chronology of events by simply analyzing the causes and effects. Then you can place the events in a chronological sequence. Any break in these causes and effects questions the chronology as premised."

What the fuck was she talking about? "So… you sell me a bullshit story and I can use cause and effect to descramble the sequence of events into a more plausible alternate theory?" I asked, trying to save my flailing dignity.

"You're such a simpleton," Ameena said good-naturedly.

"Yes, right now I am."

"You know what I'm talking about," Ameena said. I said nothing. A wise man knows when to stay silent.

We crossed the highway from the gas station. Idak Link had to be the one we could see down the hill. We walked into it right away.

"We need to hang for a bit so our contact can locate us. He said he'll be checking the road regularly. These damn busses never arrive on schedule," she said.

As we rounded the corner to the first alley, I noted that someone who had crossed the highway behind us had met up with another individual at the entry of Idak Link Road. This upcoming turn into the minor alley would be telling. Would this duo turn in with us? Or would they let a different eye take us into the alley?

Around the corner, we picked up the pace. As we turned left into another alley, I just caught a glimpse of someone entering the alley from Idak Link Road. The second alley had market vendors lined on one side. We had to confirm whether we'd actually picked up a tail or if it was just our paranoia working overtime. We still needed to get to the main road for our contact to pick us out. At the end of the block was an establishment of sorts, on our left-hand side. It looked like a hostel. Ameena gestured toward the doorway with her thumb. I nonchalantly walked inside the doorway and Ameena followed.

Just inside were a handful of older men smoking a hookah. They looked up curiously at me and Ameena. I wasn't sure if the establishment allowed women inside. As a precaution, Ameena stayed behind me. I keep forgetting that she knew this culture well. A woman inside came out from the kitchen to meet us and motioned us inside, towards a table in the back.

Just then, two men came in the doorway and sat themselves at a table across the room from us. I recognized the two men as the ones who'd joined up at the top of Idak Link Road. One male eyed us for a few seconds and nodded his head. Just then, the second male left the establishment. The woman who met us at the door served us two cups of kahwah, an Afghan tea similar to masala chai. She also served a cup to the man sitting across us.

I watched the man intently. I paid attention to where he placed his hands, whether he checked any concealed gear on himself, or displayed any unconscious discomfort from carrying a concealed weapon. You can tell from a person's body language if the person is amped up and ready to pounce. The other man soon returned with another, older man in tow. The other men in the establishment acknowledged him like an elder. The old man looked around the room at everyone. He nodded and smiled. Then he gestured toward a door along the hallway, and another fellow got up and dutifully opened it. The old man then turned to me and began to walk toward us.

He walked slowly, purposefully, and looked at us with steely grey eyes as he approached. "Ameena," he said softly. "You have come a long way."

Ameena stood up and greeted him in Arabic. "Asalaam alaikum."

The old man responded, "Wa-alaikum-salaam."

"Mister Mehdi?" asked Ameena.

"Please, call me Abu. Jabril is very fond of you. He speaks of you very highly. How was your trip?" Abubakhar Mehdi asked as he simultaneously waved his hand a single time behind his shoulder, as if to indicate to his men that all was well, and that they could stand down.

"It was long and very uncomfortable," I said. "But the land and the people are wonderful."

After the short pleasantries, Mehdi indicated that he'd like us to accompany him through the opened door in the hallway, for the requisite privacy this meeting certainly required. We followed him into a small room, and he sat himself on a chair. His men stayed outside and closed the door.

"When you go back, if you take the same route, take a proper bus," he recommended. "Just make sure you get off at Rawalpindi and find another way into Islamabad. At least you would have travelled in comfort for most of the route and still avoid the clown show with the other security services." Mehdi sounded like he was well schooled in this tradecraft.

"So. You want to know about Nasser Tushanni," he stated.

"Yes, Uncle," said Ameena. "We have heard—" Ameena began, but Mehdi interrupted her by raising his hand.

"Yes, of course. But it's late, and you need nourishment. For now, you must rest," Mehdi said. "We will continue tomorrow, *inshallah*." (God willing)

Mehdi said that there were accommodations upstairs and to make good use of them. Dinner was to be served in the next room.

"Please enjoy," he said. "Allow me the privilege of being your host. If you need anything, please speak with Fatumah, the woman who served your tea. She lives upstairs as well. And please, if you walk around Miranshah, bring one of my men with you. At all times."

Ameena quickly asked, "What do you mean by '*if* we go back'? Do you have some other destination in mind?" She sounded concerned.

"A man of peace once said, *There's nowhere you can be that isn't where you're meant to be.*" And with that, Mehdi bid us a goodnight, assuring us that he would be back the next morning.

"Wait," Ameena called after him as he turned to leave. "Which man of peace said that?"

Mehdi turned at the door to look back at Ameena. He smiled and whispered, "John Lennon."

Aside for some pakoras during a stop at one of the villages, and some lassi (a popular local drink comprised of yoghurt, water, and spices), Ameena and I hadn't eaten a proper meal since we left the Marriott in Islamabad. So when Fatumah led us into the dining area, we followed her with our appetites. Mehdi had already left the establishment with one of his men, but another stayed behind, presumably to keep an eye on us. Our dinner was a local version of shawarma that reminded me of my neighbor Abdul's cooking (although his has a distinguishably Syrian flair, and he served his up with an exotic spicy sauce).

After finishing our meals, we headed up to our rooms. The beds were more like cots, the walls were paper-thin, and the bathroom was, well, useable. It was clean, but only just. Fatumah had left a large metal pot containing boiled water (for bathing, perhaps?) that she told us was safe to drink. She said that the water supply there was good. I wasn't sure what their version of good was. Thankfully, I'd taken probiotics prior to this trip.

I didn't sleep any better than I had the night before. You know that sensation of waking up in a strange place? Well, this one knocked it out of the ballpark. I opened my eyes and on the ceiling was a gecko or house lizard staring back at me (I'll take it over a cockroach any day). My thoughts quickly turned to my usual morning routine back home: I get up early to let the dogs out to do their business; I would then take a scoop of fresh beans and put them in a grinder; then I'd allow the sound of the grinding and the aroma of the brew wash over me like a calming cloud. These were rituals that started my day. Mornings without them just didn't feel right.

I heard the faint hum of a small aircraft in the distance and reminded myself that the drones still flew here. It was a constant reminder of the tension that was here and would be again.

In these little towns, alliances ran along familial, regional, religious, and political lines. The interweaving of these ideals resulted in many combinations of collaborations and splinters. It was what characterizes day-to-day living here. Religion was discussed here with the same fervor as football in an Irish pub.

I looked out the window to see if I could spot the drone. As the buzzing sound faded into the distance, a realization ran through me that sent shivers up my spine. *I'm in terrorist country*, I thought. *How was it that I wanted to come here?*

Mehdi did not show up like he said he would the following morning. I suppose he had specifically said "*inshallah*." I took it that our morning meeting wasn't the will of the Divinity after all. Fatumah didn't know where he was. I laughed inside a bit because it was so Western of us to assume that there was a schedule for everything that occurred in this part of the world. We figured that since we were under the watchful eye of Mehdi's men that we could head out and check out the town. We just had to find that dude who followed us from the mosque yesterday. Fatumah said his name is Nurab, a distant nephew of Mehdi. He would likely be down the street towards the market, she said.

As Ameena and I headed out the door, Nurab came in from the street. Without saying a word, Nurab pirouetted around and walked out behind us. He had a smile on his face as he gestured for us to turn southward. The previous night, I watched Nurab as Mehdi was speaking, and I gathered that, although he never said a word, he understood English.

As we walked through the village of Idak, I realized that Miranshah itself was a product of a handful of smaller farming villages that had grown toward each other. But the villages had maintained their tribal feel. It felt like tribal elders still held the place together. Miranshah now belonged to the Kyber Pakhtunkhwa province of Pakistan. It is still the largest city in Waziristan and one of the largest cities of the former FATA. In 1905, the British built the Miranshah Fort so that it could govern and control Waziristan. So this place had seen its share of Western influences over the years, accommodating both Western liberalism and Islamic fundamentalism contemporaneously, swinging the pendulum from one end to the other and back again.

Nurab motioned to his wristwatch to indicate that it was time to go back. He cupped his hand and moved it toward his mouth. This was the universal gesture for eating. I was starved, so I turned around right away. I was so hungry; I would have pulled Ameena by her hair if she didn't turn around fast enough. As we walked back toward the establishment, I saw Mehdi from a distance, entering the place. I scanned Nurab for a radio or a wireless earpiece. He didn't have one. I wondered if maybe he had comms with Mehdi.

Ameena and I walked back into the hostel with Nurab behind us. The midday sun could be felt through our clothing and I was looking forward to some refreshments inside. What I felt I really needed was a beer. But we weren't on vacation here. Officially, we were on duty. No shaken martini lunches while we were on duty. Not anywhere in the world. It's so un-James Bond like. Yet the work that we did was likely the closest thing to a realistic Bond mission, less the artistic license. I did mentally note that hanging out in a hostel in Miranshah was nowhere near cruising Le Casino Monte-Carlo.

Inside, Mehdi was already seated on a table. In front of him was a glass vessel with an old-fashioned cork.

"Have a seat," he said to us as he motioned for Fatumah to bring in the food. "This is whiskey. It's not highland Scotch, but where we are, there is nothing better than Kalash." Mehdi explained that the whiskey was made by the Kalash tribe from the Khyber Pakhtunkhwa region. This is a tribe from a bygone era, a non-Muslim sect that, for centuries, was locked away by the foreboding elevations of the High Hindu Kush range. Kinda like a Shang-ri-la in the Alps of the Hindu Kush. Mehdi explained that life in the Kalash Valley was under constant threat from Muslim influences overreaching from Afghanistan and the rest of Pakistan.

"For centuries, the Kalash have made spirits. They use wine in cooking and rituals, believing that wine is purification."

I vaguely recalled somewhere in the ops manual, under foreign dignitaries, that during official dinners, members may partake in spirits while on duty. There was a small possibility that this memory could have been fabricated by wishful thinking on my part. But I wanted a shot of that whiskey, so I didn't object when Mehdi started pouring modest amounts of it into small glasses on the table. He warned us not to expect distillery filtration quality because the spirit was homemade.

"But this whiskey has pedigree," he said. Mehdi explained that Kalasha tribesmen were distinguishable in the region for their fair skin, blonde hair, and blue eyes. Some hypothesized that the Kalash tribe was of Greek origin, descendants of Alexander the Great's mighty army which made its way through here. Some anthropologists argue that the people are remnants of an Aryan migration. Notwithstanding, there is much debate on this subject. Here, in the remotest valleys of the civilized world, deep in the heart of

South Asia, you have what is ostensibly a tribe of fair skinned people remarkably unlike the rest of its South Asian neighbors. And just as remarkably, unlike their proscriptive Muslim neighbours, the Kalash made whiskey.

Mehdi raised his glass. "Cheers," he said. I recalled someone telling me that there is no toasting word in Urdu, as Muslims are not supposed to imbibe in spirits.

I was still reeling from my first gulp of the hooch when Mehdi started to speak. "Welcome again to Miranshah. I am extremely pleased that you're here. Your mission, should you accept it…" said Mehdi.

"Oh, c'mon. Seriously?" replied Ameena.

"A bit corny, I know. But this is serious stuff, and I don't know where to begin," Mehdi said. "Look, I don't want to deliberately mislead you. But angling for the truth has its rewards and its perils. I suppose it's like fishing. Some days you get the big fish, sometimes the little. But there will be times the fish get you. You've come this far in search of some explanations, yes? Well, you've come to the right place. Let's just say that today's fish is significantly bigger than what you expected to find."

Mehdi's words resounded ominously. I wasn't quite sure what he was talking about. Ameena just stared at Mehdi intently for a few seconds. Then she nodded as if she knew what Mehdi was about to say.

"You wanted to know about Nasser?" he asked. "Well, maybe it is time." Mehdi leaned forward on his elbows and cupped on hand into the other. "Yes, I know Nasser. I know Nasser very well. He and his father, Masub, we all worked together once upon a time. We were all cut from the same cloth. I wish I could distance myself and say that they were terrible people. But I was one of them many years ago. And there is nothing I could accuse them of that I haven't been guilty of myself."

"What do you mean?" I asked, leaning in.

Mehdi digressed and began telling us stories about the "golden years" of Afghanistan. He said that in the 1960's, Muslims and Jews sat together for tea. Kabul was beautiful and cosmopolitan. Tourists were enchanted by the city; they called it the Paris of Central Asia. It was unrecognizable by that description today. Kabul's entryways were now marked by American military vehicles, and wanton destruction could be found everywhere.

"I weep every night for my Afghanistan. But I cannot return. I will die far from my home and be buried on foreign soil."

Mehdi described a country that was once a pristine haven for intellects who sported a healthy passion for democratic ideals. He said that Kabul would have been a more interesting backdrop for the movie that became *Casablanca*. And it was just as exotic. I was having difficulty visualizing Mehdi's description of Afghanistan against its modern context—the war-torn, shakily governed, and bomb-pocked city so negatively portrayed by news agencies. But it had, indeed, been beautiful and peaceful once. It almost slipped my mind that this battle-worn man might have come from the elite echelons of that old country, that he may have had an Ivy League education and had come from affluence. But here he was, like his beloved country, in tatters and ruins.

He said that in the intervening years after the Second World War, Afghans were happy. It had boasted a parliament which seated more women than the United States. From 1933 to 1973, Afghanistan was ruled by a benevolent monarch, Mohammad Zahir Shah, who attempted to evenly spread power in Afghanistan. He was said to have convened a council of scholars in 1964, joined by religious and tribal leaders for the purpose of drafting a constitution that advocated for individual freedoms. But the spread of modernization was too slow, which emphasized inequities. Only Kabul benefitted from the advances, while the rural areas remained relatively conservative in their Islamic ideals and their treatment of women. Dissatisfaction grew due to slow progress, which led to a coup in July 1973.

Mohammed Daoud Khan, also born of royal blood, and cousin of the deposed Mohammad Zahir Shah, took over the government. But he was then assassinated in 1978, during the Saur Revolution led by the People's Democratic Party of Afghanistan, a communist organization (despite its name).

During his time in power, Khan pushed for progressive policies, including women's rights and Pashtun nationalism. His two- to five-year modernization plan was intended to increase the labor force by another half. It was the 1978 coup, upon Mohammed Daoud Khan's assassination, that plunged Afghanistan into a civil war. In 1979, the Soviets invaded Afghanistan and, 40 years later, Afghanistan is but a relic of its former glory.

"I am not without blame," Mehdi said. "You see, I worked with Nasser in those early years. I was misled. I thought we were working for democracy. We were working to stabilize Afghanistan, not destroy it. We were in our twenties, you see." Mehdi took a slow sip of his whiskey. "We thought we owned the world. We had money. We could travel everywhere."

In 1975, Mehdi met Nasser in the UK after they had graduated from Oxford. He said that Nasser recruited him to work for an American NGO, and so he joined Nasser during that summer. At first, they did a lot of logistics work in the name of an international aid society. It was about delivering food supplies, antibiotics, and setting up mobile inoculation clinics. They started their initiation in Africa. They cut their teeth navigating supplies into Rhodesia, and then to Asia, monitoring the Cambodian refugee camps in Thailand. By 1977, they were moving arms and ordinance into Kurdish regions in Northern Iran. As well, they worked the supply lines in Uzbekistan, Tajikistan, Kyrgyzstan, Turkmenistan, Kazakhstan, Azerbaijan, and Dagestan. There, they not only brought hardware but also propaganda material. (It struck me that the Central Asian countries he mentioned were the exact same ones Nasser Tushanni disclosed during his interview. That part on Tushanni's activities was corroborated by what Mehdi had said).

Ameena asked Mehdi how they went from delivering milk, sugar, and medicine to trafficking in arms. "Was it with the same NGO?" she asked. Mehdi said that their logistic solutions NGO was a CIA front company. He believed to this day that Nasser knew this fact at the time of his recruitment. Mehdi had been drawn into the organization without fully comprehending what its real plans entailed.

Mehdi said that Pegasus Aid International operated many subsidiaries in the region. In the late 70's, they hatched a plan to duplicate the Golden Triangle of South East Asia in the mountains of Central Asia. This is now known as the Golden Crescent. The countries that made up the Golden Triangle—Thailand, Myanmar (then known as Burma), and Laos—were, at the time, the top growers of opium poppies. Mehdi explained that the story is an old one. It started in China. It was 1949, and the US-backed Chiang Kai-shek government was overthrown by the Mao Tse Tung communist revolution. After losing the civil war, the Chiang army sought refuge in what is now the Golden Triangle. From there, with help from the governments of Thailand and Taiwan, along with the coordination of the CIA, it relaunched itself as a pro-democracy resistance movement. It backed itself with finances derived from heroin trafficking, which the CIA helped move globally. Of course, the largest consumer of the heroin was the USA. The American citizens, through pain and suffering, financed the advancement of their county's foreign policies. The Golden Crescent was named for the crescent-shaped mountainous regions of Afghanistan, Iran, and Pakistan, that still cultivate the poppy to this day.

Mehdi asked, "Who do you think operated both these triangles? There was only one common denominator—us, the CIA." I was beginning to see where Masub and Nasser Tushanni fit into this game. They managed the poppy fields on behalf of the Afghan government and the CIA.

Mehdi spoke of his experiences in Rhodesia, Thailand, and even

Kurdistan quite fondly. But when the topic migrated to the "stan" countries, I could perceive that he harbored a deep resentment against something.

After four hours of Mehdi speaking of his experiences, I wondered how much of this we would retain, especially without notebooks. Judging Ameena's conduct, it was as if she knew all this all along. That shot of Kalash whiskey went a long way with Mehdi. Mehdi's speech started to slow; it was apparent that he was getting tired. He scanned the room and nodded to Nurab. It was time for him to take a break. He slowly got up and said, "That is all for now. Please enjoy your evening. We will resume tomorrow." Mehdi asked Fatumah to serve us some tea and look after our dinner tonight.

With that, Mehdi and Nurab left the hostel. I turned to Ameena and asked if she had gotten all that. Ameena said, "I got all that a long time ago. He's just confirming what I always thought was the real story of what happened to this region."

"Explain," I said.

"Well, in our job, we write the stories that become other people's realities. This whole thing about why the Soviets invaded Afghanistan in 1979 never made any sense to me. I thought it was all fabrication. Do you remember the time when we needed to shut down 0 Avenue by Aldergrove? That was when we discovered the underground drug tunnel that led from Langley, B.C., on the Canadian side, to Lynden in Washington State. We needed a diversion to evacuate the area so we could excavate next to the tunnel and drop microphones and sensors to monitor traffic through it. So we drove a truck onto its side and simulated a toxic chemical spill. We even had a fake hazmat team there to cordon off the area. We told the media that the toxic chemicals that spilled from the truck flowed into the ditches and irrigation ponds in the vicinity.

"After about six hours, we reopened the road and assured the public that the toxic chemicals were either neutralized or recovered. Not only was that spill reported on local traffic radio, but there were helicopters feeding live news footage to national news agencies on both sides of the border. I thought to myself, *oh my fucking lord, what are we doing?* Well, that was disinformation propagated for the purpose of securing the integrity of our investigation. That incident now appears in news archives. It was pure fabrication! But now it's in archive and no one will call it into question. When we all die, that secret dies with us. It becomes verifiable history. Whether by design or afterthought, we manufactured reality. This region has been the subject of falsehoods for decades.

"I remember my first course in national security. There was this CSIS guy delivering a presentation on Islamic extremism. Dude looked like he had 12 cups of coffee during breakfast. He said that the biggest failure of the FVEY intelligence community was that they were unaware that before the Soviets invaded Afghanistan, they were already under attack by Muslim extremists. The intelligence community reported that the Soviets invaded Afghanistan for imperialistic purposes and the protraction of their communist agenda. Somehow that didn't sit well with me," said Ameena.

"What do you mean? What has that got to do with altered reality?" I asked.

Ameena said, "I'll explain this to you in time. But for now, let's wait until Mehdi tells us what we came here to learn."

I looked at the bottle of hooch Mehdi left on the table and determined that it was going to be part of my very near future. I wish I could describe what it tasted like. Being a single malt Scotch guy, my palate had some learning to do when I first ventured into Japanese whiskey (I now particularly like Hibiki and always have an open bottle at home for the casual shot). But this Kalash whiskey was far more reminiscent of those gold-medal winning rums. There was something eloquent about the note of the whiskey, despite its obvious young age; no trace of guaiacol that I could detect. I wasn't sure if the whiskey was placed in a barrel at all. I was interested in learning the process the tribesmen followed to make it, but I'd likely find little-to-no English literature about it.

Just then, Nurab came back in. I gestured that I wanted to go outside and get some air before dinner. Nurab grabbed a hookah and took it outside with us. I used to smoke when I was a teenager. That was a long time ago. Although I wasn't particularly compelled, I decided to take a few puffs with Nurab, to build some rapport. I sat there in the alleyway with him in silence, just watching people go by. No one paid any attention to us; I was just part of the scenery. Maybe the folks were just accustomed to seeing Westerners in their midst. It wasn't a big deal. Half an hour later, Fatumah came out to the doorway and gestured that dinner was ready. Nurab and I walked back into the building and I called Ameena down from her room.

It occurred to me for the seventh time since we'd been there that there was no one else in the establishment. It was like we owned the place. I didn't know what it cost us to stay there per night, or how much the meals cost. I sure hoped Ameena had enough cash. I couldn't imagine this place taking credit cards. It didn't matter whether it did or not, because we hadn't brought any. Although the people there were welcoming enough, I couldn't relieve myself of the disquieting thought that I would wake up in this foreign land with no weapons, no identification, no money, no credit cards, and no one to vouch for who I was. Other than that, I felt right at home. I just hoped the Taliban weren't in any mood to do any indiscriminate shooting.

Nurab sat down to eat with us. As he reached over for the mutton, I heard him utter an English word for the first time. "American?" he asked.

"Canadian," Ameena replied.

Nurab nodded reassuringly. Nurab had a speech impediment which, before I discerned it, I had mistaken for an accent. This was why he'd been so quiet. In his broken English, Nurab said that he used to help his uncle when he was a child, and Americans would bring him chocolate bars and toys. But then something happened.

Mehdi refused to work for them anymore. "Do you have Hershey?" he asked jokingly.

I woke up the following morning after a gloriously long sleep. I looked up at the ceiling. No geckos, no cockroaches. *Today will be a good day.* I presumed that Mehdi would show up at lunchtime again. But just after breakfast, we heard a vehicle pull up to the front door. I walked down the stairs and found Mehdi standing by the door frame.

"Good morning," he greeted. He sounded like he'd had a Milk of Magnesia morning. He said, "Today, we go on a field trip."

"Oh, a roadie," Ameena responded.

Mehdi smiled. Even his eyes smiled. It seemed as if he was instantly reminded of a moment in his youth, like the feeling of 25 years melting away for a second or two. I'm more than familiar with this feeling. The good ol' Ameena Effect.

Nurab was behind the wheel of an old 70's International Harvester Scout II. You hardly see these trucks anymore. They're absolutely classic. It was well worn but holding up pretty well. We climbed into the back seats from the front passenger-side door, as these only came in two-door configurations. When we settled in the back, I was still trying to find the non-existent seatbelt when the IH Scout II pulled away.

Mehdi said, "It's Sunday. We go to brunch and cricket in the Razmak Valley."

"How far?" I asked.

"About an hour and a half, depending on traffic."

Nurab twisted a knob on the dashboard and the radio came to life with what sounded like Pakistani pop music. Being a jazz man myself, the music sounded indistinguishable to me from the upbeat Bhangra music I'm often treated to while stopped at a traffic light in Vancouver.

Going through mountainous passes, we drove through some of

the worst chicken-gut twisties I've ever seen. In many places, the roadway literally doubled backed on itself in purchase of elevation. There were trucks and other public transport on the roadways, but there was significantly less heavy machinery on the road today than there had been when we had first entered the town. Maybe because it was Sunday. We spoke of Pakistani culture, politics, and cuisine as we cruised along—the trip was surprisingly comfortable over paved roads. I noticed that this road, in particular, seemed to have been newly paved. I mused on what it would feel like to speed down this road in a Porsche 911.

As EVO (emergency vehicle operations) driving instructors in our division, Ameena and I were especially attuned to driving conditions. We'd been teaching police officers advanced techniques for the better part of two decades. And Ameena had an even more interesting motorsports background than I did. Starting from the age of eight years, Ameena honed her competition skills in kart racing. I'm not talking about the indoor go-kart kind, with old tire barriers lining the track; I'm talking about the kinds of karts that are used for professional racing in Europe. This was a popular sport in Europe, especially in England where she went to karting school. There have been many professional kart drivers who never left the category to go to full-size cars because by the time they turned 20, they could retire altogether (and why risk having just a *mediocre* career in formula racing?). By the time Ameena was 14 years old, she was driving Formula Renault. And by 18, she was scrubbing sidewalls in the Formula 3 Race of Champions at the historic Spa-Francorchamps in Belgium.

It's too bad that automotive racing is still very much a male dominated sport. All the years I facilitated the advanced EVO driving course, I'd seen firsthand that females learned the techniques quicker because they were less hampered by testosterone in the learning process. Unlike men, women put less stock into their intuitive logic and relied more on their rational intelligence to learn the physical dynamics of driving. More importantly, they eschewed the ego game with the boys. The women were far less concerned with ultimate speed than they were of technical progress, which is exactly what mattered in my driving courses. Driving within a natural safety margin, they'd rise to display excellent technique, and eventually, were fully capable of giving the men a run for their money when speed mattered.

But every now and again, a lioness like Ameena would stroll along. She totally comprehended the engineering constructs. She used phrases like "improving human interface" and "ergonomics to extract optimal performance." One day, she brought up the fact that most American cars are ergonomically designed for men because the diameter of the average steering wheel is more representative of the width of men's shoulders. According to her, this results in less than ideal leverage for average sized women. Really? Car manufacturers are biased? In police cars, there are no side bolsters on the front seats. We wore 20 pounds of operational gear on our belts. It is a one-size-fits-all environment. Lateral support during high-g maneuvers is garnered from hand and feet placement. Along with the shoulder blades and the buttocks, these comprise the eight anchor-points that connect the driver to the car. The hands anchor on the steering wheel. It's okay if you're just bracing yourself against the wheel, she said, but if you needed turning muscle, the arms of smaller women cantilever outward, beyond the optimal angle for maximum exertion. So the solution would be to position the driver's chest closer to the steering wheel hub so that larger muscle groups could be employed. The problem is that this female-optimal position puts the air bag perilously close to a woman's face and chest. An activated airbag packs the wallop of a 12-gauge shotgun, and can knock someone out and prevent one from avoiding a potentially deadlier secondary collision. So she proposed that we order operational vehicles with gender-neutral ergonomics. When I finished laughing, I pulled her into the advanced EVO driving program straight away. Finally, here was an instructor that could still teach me a thing or two.

While she was in training academy, she beat out all the driving instructors on the serpentine track by an embarrassing margin. Those dudes realized quickly that same-old-same-old was no longer going to cut it. With her at the helm of the driver development program in B.C., we created a "skunk works" type of school for avant-garde driving techniques. The program incorporated everything from NASCAR style, use-your-opponent-for-brakes technique to police intervention techniques known as the pit maneuver. We taught ramming, boxing-in techniques, tap and tag, T-square, and a host of evasive maneuvers used by VIP motorcade teams. But mostly, Ameena incorporated the race craft braking techniques like trail, e-line, tandem, and left foot. She lectured on the value of late apexing and how it could be used for visual continuity of a suspect vehicle. She also introduced the concept of reading racing lines on commuter roadways. She completely altered the Course Training Standards (CTS). The other training divisions were lost; they just could not keep up, try as they might.

Nurab was doing some kind of skunky driving himself. He was palming the wheel all over the place, braking at the wrong time, accelerating too early, and failing to conserve the vehicle's momentum during elevation changes. He had no concept of bleeding off energy or sacrificing speed for the driving line. He entered corners too fast and exited too slow. He crossed over the median into oncoming traffic a few times and dropped the outside rear wheels into the soft shoulder constantly. It was his untidy driving technique, more than the bumpy ride, that accounted for Ameena's barely concealed winces.

Certain parts of Miranshah showed evidence of a recent battle to rid the region of TTP fighters. Some business shop lots, or strip malls had been reduced to rubble. Walls were still pockmarked with small caliber fire. Some structures stood, arbitrarily spared from destruction, amidst a sea of devastation around them. And the repaired sections of town just looked like new developments. They basically tore entire blocks down and reconstructed the buildings from the foundation up.

As we neared the venue in the Razmak Valley, we noted a lot of parked vehicles strewn haphazardly across a field. There were private cars, transport vehicles, and even military trucks. In the middle of the large expanse was a massive crowd in all manners of dress: athletic, military, business, and even indigenous attire. And the crowd surrounded a strip of grass where men in white uniforms were engaged in a game. Apparently, the local passion for cricket had never died, just as dear to the populace as before the TTP came and brought conflict to the region.

The crowd was a mix of Westerners and Asians, but the absence of women jarred me. I asked Mehdi about this and he said that it wasn't a problem, that women likely stayed away due to "disinterest in the sport," and for the same reason, didn't overwhelm mosques either. I wasn't sure if he had only answered this way to put Ameena at ease.

"We are here because I wanted to show you what these people are all about. It's more to show you what they are not. Life is simple here. They have Sunday cricket games and brunch in the marketplace. People till the soil here, and they work hard to feed their families. Politics and religion are dominant topics of discussion. But fundamentalism is not natural for them. Over the centuries, this place has been part of many empires. Even Alexander the Great and his mighty army walked through here. All those influences were from outside the region. Even the latest invaders, the TTP, had Uzbek origins. Left to their own devices, people here would play cricket. And if the Brits had not brought this game here, these people would still be here playing with sticks and stones," Mehdi proclaimed.

I got it. This place had its own equilibrium. Pakistanis, left to their own devices, would happily have this kind of contest played here on any given day. These people had been the subject of atrocities for centuries. We walked down to the field. Everyone was preoccupied with the game before them. We stayed long enough to see the first turnover, and then it was time to find something to eat. Mehdi turned to Nurab and asked him to drive us to the Cadet College. We all walked back to the car.

We stopped just short of the college at a restaurant Mehdi and Nurab obviously patronized often. We found a table outside and were instantly served tea and bread. Mehdi said that there would be no need for menus; he would order his usual fare for all of us. The proprietor brought us pata tikka and beef kebabs, the equivalent of Waziri street food. The tikka was wrapped in a layer of fat. I could feel my cholesterol rising just by looking at it, but, to be respectful, I had to try at least one bite. I knew Ameena would never touch the stuff, but she picked up a skewer and chowed down on the bits. I think Mehdi was just testing us. He just wanted to see what we were made of—for kicks. But I could tell that he was a very intelligent and intuitive person. And although he had withdrawn here in the Pakistani highlands, he came across as cosmopolitan and sophisticated underneath his traditional attire. In fact, there was even something about him that suggested secret wealth, though he seemed to have spurned luxuries for a very long time.

On the way back to Miranshah, Mehdi told us about Masub, Nasser's father. He said that Masub went to Cambridge at a time when the KGB was recruiting agents from the homosexual community there. The KGB started this program in the 30's, well before the Second World War. While they had tremendous success with their endeavors, secretly the Brits were having an intelligence coup of their own. This was all kept under wraps despite the exposé of the Cambridge 5 in the mid 50's. Yet all through this, Masub was in the periphery of attention, despite his associations with this original group. The difference was that, although the KGB initially invested in Masub, Masub did not remain in London. When he graduated in 1939, he headed to Massachusetts for Harvard, the other Cambridge, for further matriculation.

"I suspect that Masub had been debriefed by the OSS, the progenitor of the CIA, sometime during his years at Harvard. I suppose the OSS knew of his KGB affiliation in Oxford-Cambridge during those days. The OSS turned Masub, and then he later switched his allegiance to Team America. Likely, the OSS initially brought him in to ensure that he had severed his connections with the KGB.

"He is a quiet and very reserved man," continued Mehdi. "And he had a keenness for business logistics. The Tushanni family, Masub and his father, Nasser's grandfather, ran the first-ever bus line between Kabul and Kandahar. This was before the 300-mile roadway was even paved. Later in the 50's Masub's father opened an inter-Afghan air cargo company. The OSS groomed Masub for the role they intended for him." Masub was an asset ported over to the CIA when President Truman signed the National Security Act in 1947, which renamed the intelligence agency from OSS to CIA.

Mehdi said that the thesis that Masub had defended in Harvard Business School was about establishing utilities in remote outposts. It was a feat of civil engineering to unfold an operation in a remote location like one would a circus tent. But his tent would have all the amenities and utilities instantly set up from day one. That meant that he could do a quick build of a city containing X population, and scale the requirement for water, sewage and sanitation, electric power generation and storage, buildings, residences, food rations, farming implements, agricultural capacity, medical facilities, support amenities, transport and logistics, fuels, etc.

In 1949, Mao's communist revolution erupted in a civil war that unseated China's ruler, Chiang Kai-shek. The CIA contracted Masub to set up a base encampment for General Chiang's defeated army. Chiang and his loyalists fled to the tri-border region we now call the Golden Triangle. Masub operated out of Rangoon and spent two years supervising the build-up. By 1965, they were secretly producing poppy in the region. The world would not clue into this for nearly another decade and a half.

I asked Mehdi where they got the expertise to grow the crop. Mehdi said that Masub was quite the resourceful fellow. He had contacts everywhere. Since the Afghan highlands had been growing poppy for generations, there were many farmers he could contract for the project. Opium poppies had been traditionally grown in the Crescent region for far longer than in the Triangle area. But the early crops were farmed for only internal consumption. Masub changed all that. But by 1991, opium production in the Golden Crescent surpassed that of the Golden Triangle for the first time.

"Look at the statistics," Mehdi said. "The UN says that around 97 percent of opium and morphine seizures are conducted in the Middle East. So only 3 percent of heroin and morphine seizures occurred elsewhere in the world. With Afghanistan now being the top producer, where more than 95 percent of the world's opium comes from, only 1 percent of Afghan heroin is ever seized. That's everywhere around the world! One percent! Why do you think that is? And how do you think that is?"

Mehdi pushed on with his story. He said that with the success of the Golden Triangle, Masub returned to Afghanistan. Under CIA orders, he began to industrialize heroin production in the Kandahar and Helmand provinces. Masub was so clever that he convinced the Taliban to put out a *fatwa* banning the farming of opium so that he could optimize the pricing of processed heroin in the global marketplace.

But there is another player vying for the heroin trade: Iran. Iran has stakes in the heroin produced in its northern territories. So there is a high probability of heroin shipments being seized when they are smuggled from Afghanistan or Pakistan into Iran by enterprising farmers. This comprises that statistical 1 percent of Afghan heroin that is seized. The seized heroin is sold together with the rest of the Iranian heroin to the European and African markets. Hezbollah's External Security Organization (ESO) runs those trafficking operations with the full endorsement of the Ayatollah Sayyid Ali Hosseini Khamenei, the Supreme Leader of Iran.

"You saw the cricket field in the Razmak Valley?" asked Mehdi.

"Did you notice how smooth and flat that area is? That used to be our runway. Two to three times a week, a C-130 Hercules would land on that field and be packed to wing level with black heroin. We needed to move 35 metric tons a week.

"We discovered later that they flew the shipments to Ramstein Air Base in Germany. The Air Force has a strip there, just to the west of Kaiserslautern. It's better known as K-town, 80 miles southwest of Frankfurt. We only minded the acquisition; we had nothing to do with the distribution. Another subsidiary did that," Mehdi said, as if absolving himself.

This ride home seemed to take longer than the ride to brunch. Ameena sat very silently, soaking everything in. While she would be visibly curious about something in the scenery, she never interrupted Mehdi. She was always looking around and behind, to see if there was anyone expressing too much interest in us. Many times, through the mountain passes where the road doubled on itself, one could get a solid glimpse of any vehicles and occupants following behind. But nothing seemed to be out of place. Finally, I saw the Nizamia Mosque in the distance.

Nurab pulled up to the front of the hostel. Mehdi got out of his door and pulled the passenger seat up to let us out. He turned to me and said, "Finish the bottle; I'll bring you something else tomorrow." As he got back into the passenger seat, he said to Ameena, "Tomorrow, we will continue to talk about Nasser. Have a pleasant rest."

As Nurab and Mehdi slowly pulled away, Ameena and I turned to the front entrance of the hostel and were greeted by Fatumah. It was a bit early for dinner, so I headed up to my room to make copious notes of what Mehdi had said, while it was still fresh in my mind.

Just before dinner, I came down to find Ameena sitting with a couple of old men, trying to speak Arabic to them. While the first languages of these men were likely Pashtu or Urdu, there was still a good chance that one might be able to converse in simple Arabic, given that the religiously revered Quran is an Arabic document. Or perhaps Ameena was simply trying to entertain herself, or even mess with them. The conversation didn't seem to get very far, but the old men seemed to genuinely enjoy the challenge. That's Ameena for you.

Upon seeing me, Ameena politely excused herself with a "Salaam, salaam," and joined me at our usual table in the corner. Oddly, the bottle of whiskey was still there, untouched—and, conveniently, so were the small glasses. I poured out a couple shots, trying to be inconspicuous about it. I would hate to be the only infidel of the room.

"So?" I started.

Ameena just shrugged. "I feel like we're at the beginning of a journey, just like Mehdi said," she said.

"This is Alice's rabbit hole we've stumbled into. I'm afraid I already know where we're headed," I said.

"I don't want to go there," Ameena said. I agreed with her. We'd entered a house of smoke and mirrors. It was the last mirror that I didn't want to see.

This brought me back to my conversation with Ameena from the day before, about the reason the Soviets had invaded Afghanistan. We don't believe for a moment that the Soviets invaded Afghanistan for any kind of expansion purposes. From a purely economic perspective, the war would have cost them more than they could hope to gain from the territory. But they were already being hit by extremist attacks as early as the mid 70's. Or possibly earlier. But back in those days, the Soviet news agency, TASS, was highly censured by the Soviet politburo. If these attacks did in fact occur, it would not have been reported by the news agency. That being said, the CIA had sufficient HUMINT on the ground to know what colour underparts Leonid Brezhnev was wearing on any given day; I'm fairly confident that they knew whether terrorist attacks were occurring in the Soviet Union, in Moscow no less.

More likely, it was the best intelligence ruse of all time, because it only took a decade thereafter to collapse the mighty Union of Soviet Socialist Republics. In 1989, the East Berlin wall ceremoniously fell, which caused a cascading effect that saw once subordinate republics exerting newfound independence from Mother Russia.

So if the Americans lied to us about the root of the Soviet invasion, then what else did they lie about? And why would they lie about it?

It wasn't until lunchtime the following day that Mehdi returned once more to the hostel. This time he had a bottle of wine.

"Let me guess: Kalash wine?" I ventured.

"I have boxes of these. They are not bad. About the same quality as Italian house wine," he said.

Well, I thought, *then that would be more than acceptable.*

"When the hell did you start drinking, Mehdi? That's not being a good Muslim, is it?" I was trying to push him a bit to see how he would react. But he just chuckled, and in his best impression of a British accent, he replied, "In an English pub during college, ol' fruit."

"*Ol' fruit?!*" I blurted. Ameena laughed out loud. It's always good entertainment for her to see someone giving me the gears. I couldn't recall ever hearing that term of endearment before.

After lunch, we walked toward the river. It was a nice day in the sunshine, cool enough to be comfortable on a leisurely walk. By the riverbank, there wasn't another soul around. Nurab kept his distance behind us. I supposed he was allowing us our private three-way conversation.

"Did you guys also ship arms to the Afghan terrorist camps?" Ameena asked, trying to push the story ahead.

Mehdi raised his right hand, gesturing patience as he continued his story. "I told you I met Nasser in Oxford. It was my senior year. We were classmates, but oddly, I hadn't recalled ever seeing him the previous years. Maybe I had just trolled different social circles. There were many sports and extra-curricular activities, as you know. And I had liked this red-haired girl in those days and secretly followed her around campus. That consumed my early days at school.

"One day, at the resource centre, he came up to me, introduced himself as a fellow Afghan, and asked if I had a job lined up. I was actually surprised because I thought he was Persian, due to his features. There were very few Afghans in Ivy League schools anywhere in the world, and here were two of us in Oxford—and we hadn't met until our final semester! I thought that was rather strange. But here he was, asking me if I had any employment leads. I told him that I was going back to Kabul to help my father with a new business venture he wanted to start when I finished school. But Nasser was adamant; he insisted that I couldn't pass up on adventure and travel and making a lot of money while drinking my way into women's skirts. Nasser was rather flamboyant; he wasn't loud or anything, but people noticed when he was around. He was a bit of a thrill seeker, certainly. Before the month was over, we were spending most of our time together, and we quickly became best friends. How could I resist—Nasser exuded confidence and seemed to have a plan for everything. What I didn't know at the time was that he had a plan for me as well. We had this relationship in which he was like the voice, and I was like the conscience. I was the straight man to his comedy act. You know, like Abbot and Costello." Mehdi smiled briefly.

Upon graduation, Mehdi agreed to join Nasser at Pegasus Aid, delivering care packages to refugee camps in South East Asia. He didn't know then that it was his initiation, a test of his mettle, and his limits. The Agency was grooming them, scrutinizing them for future missions. They had the same "handler," a Major Jim Cunningham from Dallas, Texas. Major Cunningham supervised them through their early days in Thailand. Mehdi called him "FedEx" because he always said "our shipments absolutely, positively needs to get there!" Cunningham was a real social worker, a salt-of-the-earth type of guy. But soon, Cunningham handed them over to Faizal for the Central Asian operations.

By the summer of 1976, they found themselves operating out of a merchant vessel in the Caspian Sea. They were a covert supply vessel shipping aid supplies to the Kurds in North West Iran, and arms and ordinance to the shores of Dagestan, Azerbaijan, Turkmenistan, Uzbekistan, and Kazakhstan. These were mature and well-established supply lines that had been in operation for years before Mehdi's time. The CIA had signals intelligence assets that wound their way up and down the Caspian, monitoring all manner of radio communications. They had secret technologies on board, dilapidated-looking freighters and fishing trawlers.

"We bought Semtex and Type 56 Chinese AKs and stored them in armories all over the region. The best source during those days was none other than Adnan Khashoggi, the infamous international arms dealer. Nasser, of course, came from a logistics family. His creation was the overland supply line to ship materials to Kyrgyzstan and Tajikistan from Afghanistan. When Nasser was away looking after the overland shipping, I had to manage the marine activities by myself—although now and again, Faizal would be there to help if I got overwhelmed.

"You see, these republics harbored resentment towards the Russians for occupying their lands. This was the premise behind the CIA targeting 6 of the 15 Soviet republics, selecting those whose populations were predominantly Muslim. My syndicate and I delivered anti-Soviet propaganda and provided the weapons cache meant for the inevitable, asymmetrical warfare. We selected and trained political officers and religious leaders."

"Political officers?" Ameena asked.

"Yes," Mehdi replied. "The Russians used *zampolits*, political commissars, to keep people towing the political line. It was before my time, but our operatives established core resistance groups in the Stans. But because the people had gotten accustomed to Soviet structures, the Agency recruited and trained political commissars to advance and strengthen resistance propaganda. We socially engineered both the political and religious ethos of the Stans."

So, this was the deployment of the divide-and-conquer strategy to take down the mighty Soviet Union. Mehdi said that these Stan republics were all marginalized economically. Under the Soviets, the elites were comprised of those that had favourable ranking in the communist party system. So the Soviets incentivized membership, and especially leadership, in the communist party. *Zampolits* were utilized to maintain the standards and consistency of political ideology espoused by the Kremlin. The Agency needed to create incentives of their own. The operations started under the cover of benevolent foreign aid. It was very low key in the beginning; the operatives could not afford to attract any kind of attention from the communist authorities. In the early stages, the operatives trafficked only in grains, bread, and halal meats. They distributed the most basic of necessities to create a network upon which to build their resistance movements.

Mehdi said that the Agency was also engaged in the Baltic region. There, operatives brewed local dissent, reignited the fire of nationalism, and mobilized independence movements in the three Baltic states: Lithuania, Estonia, and Latvia. They figured one of them might eventually flare up in the future. Of course, the objective to all this was to destabilize the Soviet Union from within; namely, if the USSR was too busy fighting internal battles, it would drain its dwindling resources and handicap it for the competition that mattered most to the US and its allies: the nuclear race. Of course, there were other ways of achieving destabilization—say, an economic downturn that would, in turn, lead to civil unrest. This diversion would be significant enough to tip the advantage over to the US and NATO.

The Baltics already had an ongoing resistance movement left over from the mid-50's, the Forest Brothers guerrilla force. It was a partisan response to the Soviet invasion and occupation of Latvia, Estonia, and Lithuania during and after WWII. There, the seat of resentment never really cooled. And there was a need to keep those embers burning. The Baltic makeup is markedly different from the Stans; firstly, the dominant religion is Christian, with Catholic and Lutheran making up the largest proportion. Their basic needs were also different; there, the aid consisted mostly of items like toilet paper, sanitary napkins, soap, and basic food stuff like grains, flour, and even potatoes.

The Soviets had a good track record for quelling rebellion. In 1956, the pro-Soviet government in Hungary lost, and the incumbents intended to withdraw Hungary from the Warsaw Pact. The Soviets then needed to invade Hungary to prevent it from seceding. The Goryani movement in Bulgaria, between the late 40's and mid-50's, the Romanian anti-communist movement which lasted into the 60's, the Belarusian Independence Party, the Chechens, Moldovan, Polish, and Ukrainian resistance movements all petered out. The US—or, more specifically, the CIA—was committed to bringing the Soviets something that they could not readily dismiss.

They established weapons caches in the Stans and loaded their magazines with explosives for when they might be needed. The Agency knew that the KGB was doing the exact same thing, loading up reserves in Finland, Switzerland, and Denmark. It was the Soviets who were backing the Red Brigades in Italy, the German Red Army, and indirectly, the Palestinian Liberation Organization. The Soviets wanted to use the Reds to destabilize Italy and Germany, to break up NATO, just as they suspected the US of having done with Poland and Hungary, to weaken the Warsaw Pact.

There was going to be an all-out party, and the CIA was hosting. Everything was funded by what would become nearly 90 percent of all the heroin and morphine traffic on the planet, and then some. A lot of money moved about for these operations to succeed. There were fixed costs that needed to be maintained for safe houses, bribes for officials, storage facilities, aid products, propaganda material, vehicles, and vessels. It was just as expensive to engage in a covert war as an overt one. The support services were beyond imagination: nuclear submarines, TK resources, 24/7 surveillance missions both on the ground and in the air, AWACS and F-14s overwatch just across the nearest friendly border, etc. The black book accounts that the Finance Committee often jeered about were continuously draining, and no one outside of Langley's sphere of influence had any clue as to where the funds were going. The Agency was ready with the how.

It just needed to spark a why. It needed to convince the respective nationalists to proceed with the plan and to do it now.

According to Mehdi, by around 1978, Nasser had returned to Afghanistan while he was still doing the milk run in the Caspian. What Mehdi later learned was that Nasser went to work in Masub's syndicate. His task was to create 6 mobile paramilitary training camps in remote locations that were serviceable by air. Each camp conformed to the parameters his father designed, similar to those Masub created in the Golden Triangle. But these needed to dismantle quickly, to change locations on a second's notice. There were no permanent sewage lines. And the locations needed underground spring water. Everything else could be flown or trucked in. The Agency provided the military instructional resources. Initially, the program was about "training the trainers." The instructional staff was the who's who of Soldier of Fortune. At that time, the trainees themselves were mercenary types, motivated only by money. And the course content was on guerrilla warfare on the one hand, and improvised weapons training on the other. The guerrilla techniques were little more than terrain adjusted Vietnam-era warfare. In those early days, improvised devices were restricted to relatively high safety and reliability ordinance. Booby traps were remote or trip-wired claymore mines, hand grenades, and C-4 clay with initiators. What evolved decades later as IEDs were products of anarchist cookbook stuff that eventually permeated the Internet. But these camps were about knowledge transfer to the trainers of the actual fighters. These camps were meant to close down and then reopen across the vast expanse of the Stans.

The first batch of trainees came from all over the Islamic world. There were Arabs, Central Asians, Africans, South East Asians, and Europeans. Mehdi said that in the Islamic world, there was no such thing as a "foreign fighter;" in ancient times, the Islamic world was one nation. The concept of fighters travelling across territories like what ISIS did over the northern Arabian Peninsula follows from ancient convention. When Saladin took siege of Jerusalem in 1187, his army was partly comprised of fighters from what is now Egypt and Syria. Saladin himself was a Sunni Kurd. Whatever was going on in the paramilitary training camps looked like the perfect formula for what would later define Islamic jihad in the 21st century.

As we walked back to the hostel from the riverbank, I asked Mehdi if the Soviets had an ear up on CIA activities in Afghanistan. He said, "Sure. We had our spies, they had theirs. It was like a cat and mouse game. You know, cloak and dagger. I still think that they got nervous enough about our activities here that they sanctioned the assassination of Mohammed Daoud Khan in 1978. They invaded Afghanistan the following year in 1979 because of our success in the Stans. They had no choice. It was a checkmate situation for them."

"What happened in the Stans?" I asked.

Ameena interjected. "What happened is that, as far back as the mid-70's, Muslim operatives had been conducting sabotage operations inside of Russia, right down into Moscow. Nasser's recently built training camps were no longer meant to train insurgents in the Stans; they were meant to prepare *mujaheddin* for the Soviet invasion."

Mehdi turned to her, surprised. "Oh, you have game. This is very fortunate. *Allah* has chosen a worthy jihadist." Mehdi had a big smile on his face.

Nothing about Ameena surprised me anymore. But this was the first inkling I had that maybe there was a different reason for our being here. I could barely recall the rationale we wrote on the ops plan we submitted a week and a half ago. I had a sinking feeling that our original reasoning was about to pale into nothing more than pretense. Whatever we uncovered here, I hoped it would be a chargeable criminal offence, because otherwise, we'd be in trouble. For the first time in my career, I could feel Lorne's boot on my ass. Notwithstanding, this was still a national security matter, and my ass was on this file.

Was Nasser Tushanni facilitating, providing material support for, financing, or enabling a terrorist entity, person, or organization? I needed to break this down for myself. These activities Mehdi described occurred back in the 70's. That put it about 30 years before Canada's Anti-Terrorism laws. It's not a retroactive piece of legislation, although there is extra-territorial jurisdiction if a person is Canadian or a resident of Canada when it was committed. That means that we could theoretically charge a Canadian, or a Canadian residing in Canada, for committing a terrorist offence on foreign land. But I needed a recent offence.

Nothing here equated to an actionable terrorist offence yet. And so far, no drug charges could be advanced either, because Canada cannot assert jurisdiction over a narcotics distribution offence that occurred elsewhere, not even if the perpetrator is Canadian. Nasser did not ever traffic drugs into Canada. Canadian courts assert author-ity over some offences that occurred outside of Canada. These are a construction of offences that lend extraterritorial jurisdiction. Sex crimes, including the gamut of child exploitation offences, are the most regularly enforced ones. Terrorism, human trafficking, and hostage taking are also included. And there are offences committed by public service employees and offences against cultural property. There are some offences, like torture, where very specific circum-stances must be present for extraterritoriality to apply. It's all fairly complex, but it's good to know them, as they avail one of investiga-tive avenues.

I asked Mehdi how he had managed to fall into the disfavour of the Taliban. He said that his troubles did not originate with the Taliban; rather, it was his falling out with the Tushannis. Because Masub was an overlord, his underling tribal elders felt compelled to mirror his displeasure with Mehdi.

"They betrayed our cause," he said. "But more importantly, they betrayed Afghanistan. I'll never see Afghanistan restored to its former glory. Not in my lifetime."

"There's always hope," I said.

"Not for me," said Mehdi. He dismissed Nurab, who was walking closely behind us, and went right into it. "I have pancreatic cancer," he said. "I will not be around this time next year, maybe not in six months. I thought it quite timely, Jabril telling me about your inquiry about Nasser. It is as if it were meant to be."

"Does he—" Ameena started to ask, but Mehdi cut her off.

"He knows nothing of this. He is a good boy. I don't have children, but I love him as if he was my own son. Uncle Abu, he calls me. I was his hero when he was a child. That's why he's with the CIA. He earned his own way there; I didn't pull strings for him. He didn't need it. I'm so proud of him. One day, he will know what his hero did. I hope he judges me fairly.

"I hope the world judges all of us fairly," he continued. "You know, I welcome my judgement. I was almost glad when the doctor in Paris told me about my condition. After receiving the news, the first thought that entered my mind was that *Allah* chose to take me, the one with the conscience. But I am comforted by the fact that I do not have much longer to live with my regret for my part in all this."

"I'm so sorry," said Ameena. "Is there something we can do?"

"You tell the story," Mehdi said.

"I don't understand," Ameena replied. "How? Hasn't much of this been written by analysts and academics in the past already? People know about the opium, Chiang's army, and the Golden Triangle. They know about the CIA's Taliban, the Golden Crescent. Maybe not the fact that you pre-empted the Soviet invasion, but look at what happened in the Iran-Contra Affair—what did it change? They found themselves a scapegoat and everything went back to same old, same old."

"But this is just the beginning," Mehdi said. "The story goes on much longer. You will not learn all of it from me. Don't worry; you will be able to validate your story as you go along. I will make sure of it. You need to go to Belarus and then the Sudan."

"I don't know how we can," Ameena replied. "We're already outside of mandate here. We need to be back in Vancouver by the end of the week. Our investigation concludes here."

I could hear Ameena utter those words, but her body language said something else. I could tell that her brain had already started crunching the numbers. While her lips were saying no, her mind was trying to figure out a way to say yes.

"*Ameena al-Amine.*" Mehdi spoke her full name is if it were poetry and smiled. "Your family is all about justice. Your father was an activist for democracy. I don't think you knew that. Your grandfather authored jurisprudence in the pre-eminence of the late Justice Oliver Wendell Holmes Jr. This thing is in your blood. Do you not yearn for a fair world?" Mehdi was pushing now. Ameena was surprised by Mehdi's turn.

"What do you know of my family?" she asked.

"I know of your grandfather, Ameena. I sat beside him at a state dinner in Rabat many years ago. You are a family of warriors. All you need is a worthy cause. Be the hand that bears *Allah's* sword."

"There is no way my boss will allow this investigation to proceed. We're already off the grid coming here. If we don't report back by tomorrow night, we would be declared AWOL or missing, and then they'll start a search for us," Ameena said. "The second thing is that we used our diplomatic passports to get here. We didn't carry our personal passports with us." Clearly Ameena has already started working out the possibilities.

"Ah, but you underestimate me. Nurab here isn't just a pretty face. He'll have Canadian passports for you under different names. And he'll hand you active credit cards in those names. The cards are backed by a couple of RBS accounts in London, with a hundred thousand pounds sterling between them. Use them for everything you need, flights, hotels, taxis, and incidentals. You have no extra clothes with you. Get some," Mehdi encouraged gently.

"Why? What is it we would find?" Ameena asked.

"There are some things that you will have to see firsthand. I'm sending you to Belarus. There you will meet Panther; she worked our Saudi bureau. She has her own piece of the story to tell.

Panther was the architect of the Agency recruitment in the AP, the Arabian Peninsula."

"In Belarus?" I asked.

"She retired there. She is one of the lucky ones. She found love and raised a family away from the cesspool we created," Mehdi said. "Panther is an American. Once upon a time, she was a hard-ass operative, one of our best. You would've liked her, Ameena, she was feisty. You'd still enjoy her, surely, but today, we're just tired, old warriors with large pits of regret in place of stomachs."

"Why are you bringing this out now?" Ameena asked, "Because you're dying? Won't this just expose the ones who will still be around to suffer the consequences? Like Panther?"

"We think the clock has started ticking again," said Mehdi. "We got word that Faizal Reza, our old handler, was killed by a bomb someone had planted in his car. Faizal retired in Cairo under an assumed name. He is a very astute operator. He doesn't make mistakes. We are certain that he has not made any new enemies since."

"But why now?" Ameena asked again. "After all this time? What's changed?"

"We don't know for sure. We think that some of the old alliances we forged have changed. And perhaps the new arrangement needs to clean up old tracks. We don't know who is behind it yet. I am afraid to say that you might have some exposure here. Nothing is gained without some risk," said Mehdi.

"We can take care of ourselves," Ameena replied.

Really? I thought to myself. But certainly it was too late to back out now. Ameena would go do this herself, I was sure of it. And I couldn't let her go at it alone. The right thing to do would be to opt out right at this very moment. But that wasn't likely to happen here.

"There is a satellite phone in the car. Call your LO in Islamabad," Mehdi said as he motioned to Nurab to approach.

I looked at Ameena. I saw the unmistakable determination in her eyes and sighed. *Here we go.* "Maybe we could burn off some leave time to do this mission. If we can get the trip done inside of a couple of weeks," I offered her. Because this would be an unauthorized foray into the unknown, it would have to be done on our own time and at our own risk. Normally when we travelled for work, we had to carry along a card that says that the Canadian government guarantees to pay compensation for any necessary medical services provided to its employees. I wondered if we could get medical insurance coverage for this unauthorized trip. I asked Mehdi about it and he chuckled.

"You're not in the US," he said. "Medical treatment is not that expensive around here. Besides, you have your credit cards. Use those if you have to." Something Canadians learn from frequent shopping forays across the US border is to never take travel medical insurance for granted.

Ameena contacted the Islamabad embassy. The LO was quick to let her know that we had him worried. He said that we had skipped town without a security detail and that we should head back in right away. Ameena just asked him to advise EHQ that we would be away for a couple of weeks on our own time. Ameena thanked the LO for his help on the file and then ended the call abruptly. It was important to leave out details and deprive other intelligence agencies a convenient way of tracking us. There was no doubt that even the LO's phone was compromised. In this region, all cellular activity was monitored. The extremist groups must have been on to this, because they began employing their own encryption systems. If it comforted them any, then I was glad. Those encryption algorithms were child's play for the likes of Jabril and his team. What made them think that the encryption software sold to them didn't already have a solution in the NSA's holdings? When I asked Mehdi about communication, he said that his satellite phone was relayed to a "dumb" cell phone in Rawalpindi. It was likely triangulated but it had no significance; they weren't looking for it. After the call to the LO, he had to text someone to scrap the burner and reactivate a new one elsewhere.

The plan was for Nurab to get us across the Afghan border and into Kabul. The Hamid Karzai International Airport was a half-hour closer than Islamabad from Miranshah. There were no direct flights from Kabul to Minsk. With a single stop in Istanbul, it would take nine hours by air. Ameena would carry a burner phone, and she would receive instructions on that phone as to where to meet with Panther. But for now, we needed to memorize our cover stories before we crossed the border. Mehdi said that the Karzai airport had been renovated a few years ago and that, *inshallah,* the Wi-Fi works as advertised now. He told us to use online booking for our accommodations in Minsk. He had already taken the liberty of arranging our meeting with Panther, he said with a mischievous grin; in fact, it had all been arranged before we had even left Canadian soil.

Within the hour, we were on our way to Kabul. Nurab drove like his hair was on fire. This was of concern to Ameena and I, because bad driving done fast ends bad real fast. Those are words to live by, literally. In 35 minutes, we covered the 20 or so miles to the Ghulam Khan border crossing. Averaging 40 miles an hour on the Bannu-Miranshah is a feat on its own. Luckily, traffic was cooperative. Even luckier, I thought, was that the border was open. There are times when the border crossings are shut down. In 2017, the borders were shut down for 22 days due to armed clashes. Now Pakistan was building a 900-mile fence. I wondered where they got that idea from. They had already dug a 1,100-mile trench in the Balochistan region to control cross-border traffic from Afghanistan.

The crossing was a non-event. It looked like the border officers on either side may have recognized the IH Scout and waved it through after peeking inside a few times. My experience tells me that, sometimes, easy comes at a cost. In this cloak-and-dagger world, you never know what to expect. I asked Ameena what she envisioned we were going to find at the end of this journey. The Sudan seemed to be a rather strange and distant destination. I wondered what possible connection it had to our investigation.

Ameena said that in January of 2019, newspapers published that

President Trump had blurted out that the reason the Soviets had invaded Afghanistan was because they were being targeted by terrorist attacks. That started a massive back-pedaling in the Senate and the military. When the Soviets entered Afghanistan, the first thing they did was take out the remote paramilitary training facilities.

"Sound familiar?" Ameena asked.

"They needed to take Nasser out," I said.

"Exactly," she replied. She said that since WWII, the US had been continuously engaged in armed conflicts around the globe. First it was Korea. Then they initiated a secret war in Vietnam. Then there were more secret wars in Laos and Cambodia. Some wars were fought by proxy and some with US troops. Even the CIA was running an army and had taken on mercenary soldiers. The Special Operations Command (SOCOM) stated that US Special Operations forces were, as of 2013, deployed in 143 countries. Are we seeing a pattern here? In 2012, the US engaged in a proxy war against Iran's IRGC Quds Force in Syria. Sadly, for US defense contractors, the Ayatollah did not have a tremendous amount of disposable resources and couldn't go toe-to-toe with them. What the US needed was for Putin to come out to play so that another Vietnam-era defense budget could be justified. For now, the US continues to engage in smaller theatres to keep the coffers happy. Right now, they're fighting not-so-secret wars in Africa.

"Do you remember my security assessment of the Nineveh Governorate in March of 2014?" Ameena asked.

It was a rhetorical question. Of course, I recalled it. That was a time when ISIS had been decimated and no longer had two cents to rub against each other. We were looking at coalition resources on the ground in Mosul. The undefended border with Syria lay only 66 miles to the north. And there were no points of defense anywhere along the route. We assessed that the Iraqi coalition forces would quickly disperse at first contact with ISIS. The Iraqi forces were rumored to have not been paid wages for months. We had doubts that their loyalties would stand. You see, they were former Iraqi regular forces. They used to work for the Baathist generals, then allied with Abu Bakr al-Baghdadi. We suspected that the Iraqi coalition forces would refuse to fire their weapons against ISIS. They did not. They simply switched sides and got paid. The US analysts must have come up with the same assessment that we did. Sure enough, with no resistance, ISIS marched down the Nineveh corridor in June and took control of coalition assets parked in Mosul. I should say they were State Department spec assets, the now iconic white Toyota pickup trucks along with caches of weapons and ordinance. By August of 2014, news reports from the region stated that ISIS took the Bank of Mosul for $172 million. We could almost hear them singing "Happy Days Are Here Again."

The subsequent weeks were telling because, almost immediately, the contractors were knocking on Congress' door saying, "Oh look, they took your weapons. I guess you'll need to order more from us." I noted a tinge of sadness in Barack Obama's face that week, as anyone could see that he was not in control of that country. There needed to have been some outside interference in the Mosul strategy; US intelligence is anything but incompetent. But where would the interference come from? Therefore, conspiracy theorists speculate on a cabal, a secret society of sorts that wields the real decision-making power in America. If one could follow the money, I'm sure that it would just lead to the usual list of suspects.

Going back to Trump's comment on the invasion of Afghanistan, I seriously believe he had seen the briefing note on it but had forgotten that it was supposed to be top-secret. When he made that comment, almost immediately, detractors were on his case, academics, military specialists, etc. You see, the official story line is that in 1979, the new Afghan president, Hafizullah Amin, wanted to improve US-Afghan relations. To support this, the state department supposedly surfaced a cable from a US diplomat to Washington that stated that Amin was warming to the US. Leery that the US was courting

Amin to good effect, the Soviets decided to invaded Afghanistan and route America's political advances. I am sure that was an official memo from a US diplomat that had leaked itself to the Soviets, right? And of course, the CIA had nothing to do with it. The CIA had nothing whatsoever to do with the smothering of Amin's predecessor with a pillow, either. Just saying. To settle this Soviet invasion debate, someone should just try to locate a few Russian witnesses to these alleged extremist attacks and settle the issue once and for all.

OFF TO MINSK 6.

Hamid Karzai International Airport was looming ahead. We put together some bags to look like normal luggage for two backpackers. Ahmed Wali Karzai, the president's father, was a godfather of the Afghan underworld. He was killed by an associate in 2011 in a murder-suicide. According to the New Yorker, "Karzai cavorted with drug dealers, oversaw gangs of gunmen, and made deals with the very Taliban insurgents the Americans were trying to kill." They named an airport after his son. They sound like another Masub and Nasser father and son team, don't they? I'll let you guess who they were working for.

At the gate, Ameena and I bought tickets from KBL to MSQ on Turkish Airline. I asked the airline folks for direct flights I may have missed online, but there were none to be had. The flight we purchased stopped in Istanbul. It would take us 28 hours to arrive in Minsk from here. We purchased business class tickets so we could use the lounge. Western food and a hot shower had been a real luxury on this trip so far. I didn't usually look for burgers, but I was happy to have one for my next meal. We checked in through security and headed to the lounge. We needed food, a cleanup, and Wi-Fi to book accommodations in Minsk. This was the newer terminal. The old terminal took on the domestic traffic. While small by international standards, the airport was clean, and the Wi-Fi worked. We bought appropriate clothing at the duty-free and stowed our traditional Pakistani garb. I wondered how James Bond managed to keep himself looking immaculate despite never carrying any luggage.

After we showered and changed, we waited in the lounge seating area. Seated across from us was a middle-aged South Asian man speaking to someone on his cellular phone. He held up the phone in front of his face, as many people do when using the speaker function during a call. But when Ameena stood up to retrieve a magazine, I noticed from the corner of my eye that the man's cell phone was tracking Ameena's progress across the seating area, and then back again.

Now, I'm paid to be paranoid, but since the advent of cellphone HD cameras, taking up-close surveillance photos of targets has become much easier. There is no longer a need for miniature cameras or bulky telephoto lenses. You can mount a GoPro camera inside any common item like a milk carton, then poke a pin hole for the lens. The phone app can control the camera remotely. I've seen people use helmet cams in some situations, taking covert photos in an overt manner. The magnitude of surveillance that people are exposed to daily is alarming.

I grabbed my personal cell phone from my bag and turned it on while still in the bag. It was still on airplane mode with the Wi-Fi turned off so it wouldn't ping its IMEI or MAC address. I turned on the video recording and simply waved the phone around inconspicuously. I could later take screenshots of the video and edit the stills to isolate the target. I whispered to Ameena and gave her a heads up. She waited five minutes and then jumped up to greet a patron who had just entered the lounge. She spoke to him in Italian and pretended to have been expecting him. Just then, the middle-aged man raised his cell phone again, presumably to take a photo of Ameena's new friend. Quietly, in Arabic, Ameena apologized to the new patron and Ameena retired to the women's washroom. She simply confirmed what I suspected. I transferred the photo to Ameena using a memory card. Maybe Mehdi's network could identify the man.

As we headed to our boarding gate, Ameena turned on Mehdi's

burner phone. She sent him a text about the possible surveillance burn. Mehdi typed back, *NDS watches foreigners. Keep heads up.* NDS is the Afghan National Directorate of Security that had replaced KhAD, the KGB-supported intelligence bureau during the Soviet occupation. At boarding, there was a uniformed officer, possibly military, examining documents at pre-boarding. He was asking questions of passengers lined up for the flight. As Ameena stepped up to board, another officer approached and asked me for my passport. The first officer asked, "Purpose of visit to Afghanistan?"

"Business," Ameena said instantaneously. "Mining consultants for AGMC," she continued, sticking to the cover story.

"Where were you staying?" the officer asked.

"Safi Landmark," Ameena responded.

"And where is that?" the officer continued to question her.

"Downtown, on Shahid Road." Ameena was lightning quick but very nonchalant.

"Where is your luggage?" the second officer asked me.

"We have permanent accommodations there, a second home," I said.

"What is your title?" he pressed further.

Ameena addressed both officers and said, "We are mining engineers." She reached into an outer pocket of her backpack and retrieved a security tag with AGMC written on it. There was even a photograph of her. The second officer took both passports and examined the visas. The officer handed us our passports back and motioned us forward.

We got on the plane and, to my disappointment, discovered business class on Turkish was like Premium Economy on budget Canadian airlines. The 737-800 had the standard three and three rows, but in the forward business section, the middle seats were simply blocked off. I had hoped for more leg room on this hop.

Priority boarding is great in the context of counter-surveillance. You can scan and observe all the passengers as they board. Having surveillance on an aircraft with a scheduled destination is next to useless for anything other than overhearing conversations, and the odd time that electronic surveillance can be utilized. Most people turn off their phones during a flight. But budget flights are increasingly utilizing the passenger's own mobile devices for inflight entertainment. This renders a device that is captive for hours, vulnerable to attacks using Wi-Fi exploitive techniques.

Ameena and I carried our Faraday bags with us. They shielded the phones from external signals. Notwithstanding, we didn't keep anything on our phones that was of value anyway. We had our contact numbers, but our work e-mail content wasn't stored on the mobile devices. In this day and age of Access to Information and Privacy requests, the public can simply access the contents of our devices upon request, so long as it meets the RCMP's criteria. So only fools mess around on work devices. Sadly, there's never a shortage of them.

The six-hour flight to Istanbul was otherwise uneventful, but the almost 22-hour layover was near distressing. We had no desire to hang around the Istanbul Airport, as new and interesting as the place was. The old Ataturk International Airport had closed, and it was replaced by this new one closer to the north shore of the Euro-Asia "bridge." The city is now about 45 minutes away from the heart of town. I thought it was time to do some exploring and a bit of counter-surveillance, cat-and-mouse style, about town.

I used my credit card and took out some Turkish lira at the currency exchange. While still in the secured section of the airport, I rented two portable Wi-Fi routers for the day. Then Ameena and I took a shuttle bus into downtown so that anyone tailing us wouldn't inadvertently lose us in Istanbul traffic. We grabbed a Dosso Dossi Hotels & Spa bus to get us into town. We latched onto the mobile Wi-Fi routers and created virtual Viber telephone number accounts and put each other's numbers in our contact books. From the hotel, we would take public transit to the Grand Bazaar and clean off inside. There is much the mouse can learn about the cat during a chase.

The bus pulled up to the hotel and I tipped the driver 100 lira for both of us. God bless 4G and Google Maps. We walked to a corner stop just across the hotel and took the R3 bus heading to the Grand Bazaar. Easy as pie. No guesswork.

We got off the transit bus a few blocks from the bazaar and walked the rest of the way in. Google directed us to a stop that fed conveniently into the Beyazıt Gate along Kalpakcılar Caddesi. The Grand Bazaar is one of the biggest and oldest covered marketplaces in the world. For numbers, you're looking at 330,450 square feet of 64 covered streets and alleys, squeezing in 4,000 shops. This mall has 22 entrances. Its tight confines are a nightmare for foot surveillance, should anyone dare. *Let's see what today's cat is made of.*

The first thing we needed was dinner. Eating is a great static activity to pick up heat, if it is around. The best practice for a watcher is to hold a target in a crowded environment like the Bazaar, maintaining a constant eye on the target. But if the area is too tight, to avoid a burn, a team might just opt to hold the target locked inside a control perimeter. This second option covers the egress points but loses the direct line of observation to the target. So while ordering Turkish coffee at the stand, we had to take inventory of persons that would have an eye on us. At this point in the game, anyone wanting to watch us would have no clue as to what we are up to. They would just be collecting information. So they would want to hold us, loosely avoiding a burn this early in the exercise. Knowing the exact surveillance objective now provides us with some advantage we did not have before. Additionally, if Ameena and I split up, it would also halve their surveillance resources and cut its efficacy in half. So, in this maze of stores and vendor stands, we first needed a lay of the land to map out our trap.

This bazaar is famous for many things—tourists getting lost inside, or losing their bearings, were common occurrences. The English-language tour card that I had picked up at the entrance recommended that new visitors choose just one exit and then work a limited area in proximity to that exit. It further suggested that visitors reacquire their bearings on the outside of the marketplace, and then follow the same procedure for the next exit. Alternatively, visitors could simply enjoy the thrill of getting lost—but it's not an efficient way of maximizing your time in this place. There is too much to process in the Grand Bazaar. One could walk around in circles all day long.

After dinner, Ameena and I started walking around and memorizing the main roads and a few alleyways. I saw far too many people to be able to recall. We saw shops that had mirrors on display, up front or on their back walls. These were great for holding a "reverse eye" on targets. On the other hand, they helped us keep track of our tails. This was a game of who's up on their tradecraft. We held conversations with other tourists and non-vendors in order to shift attention to those people. Then we returned to our first restaurant and Ameena drew the game plan on a napkin.

The first thing we identified was the dead ends. You don't lose your target at a dead end, so watchers won't typically follow a target down a dead end. Even if visual continuity is broken, reacquisition of the target is almost certain because there's only one way out. So we would stay on the narrow throughways, split up, and double back toward each other; then we'd return to a specific spot and see who got trapped in between. It would also be wise to use the video camera apps on our phone, as an aid. Then we could review the footage afterward.

We do not practice counter-surveillance enough, I reflected. In fact, I don't believe there is a training course on it anymore, under the auspices of the Federal Training Branch. Shame.

At the leather shop entrance called Bitpazari, we split up. I went towards the jeans section at Yarim Tashan and Ameena paralleled on Sipahi Street. Six blocks up, we retraced our steps back to each other. The rule is, if targets split up and rejoin, on the next take away, surveillance resources change to a different target to reduce the risk of being detected. We could only do the double back once, because then our watchers would know that we were on to them and we had conducted a "heat check." But, if done just once, it could be chalked up to coincidence. On my way towards Ameena, she sent me a Viber message which read, *T1 M 25 Brn/Hzl 178 82 grey scarf whi/blk.* This meant that she had identified a possible Target 1, and described him as a male, approximately 25 years old, with brown hair, hazel eyes, 178 cm in height, 82 kg in weight, wearing a grey scarf on a white top with black pants. On my double back, I recognized this male when we crisscrossed in a small alleyway. *Good*, I thought. *Now to reverse the role and follow you back, buddy.*

The inner Bedesten was like a miniature plaza in the Grand Bazaar. This was an area for vendors who sold antiques and copper wares. As we slowly cornered T1, who was nonchalantly moving further away on a third axis as we approached from opposite directions, we went into mirrored shops and reverse-eye videoed the street. Eventually, T1 walked out one of the other gates and we walked around to see more of the shops, this time, just for our personal gratification. We weren't concerned about what surveillance of us would garner, since we weren't exactly doing anything. But to know that we were being watched introduced a new dimension into this game.

Later in the evening, we sat at another coffee shop and compared videos. There were two people that were captured in more than one location. A second male showed up on several reverse-eye videos. He seemed to have a long eye from across the road looking towards Ameena after the split, and then at me after we crisscrossed. I called him the Sultan because, minus the headwear, his long traditional shirt and white beard made him look like one. We extracted some stills of T1 as well as the second male, T2. Ameena turned on Mehdi's burner phone and reported that we could have picked up interest when we landed in Istanbul. Mehdi asked for us to Viber the photos to him at a virtual number he was texting over.

We took a cab back to the airport. It was getting late and we thought that the only rest we would get was in the lounge. All I could think of was the fact that by this time tomorrow, I'd be fast asleep at the Renaissance in Minsk. Not as good as my bed at home, but more than acceptable. I could almost smell the clean sheets and crisp white towels.

The following morning, we continued into the second leg of the journey. It took a little over two and a half hours, point to point. At Minsk National Airport, we took out a couple of Wi-Fi routers again and figured out how to clean ourselves off before going into the Renaissance. Just as we stepped outside the secure area onto the public side of the terminal, Ameena received a Viber message from Mehdi asking her to phone him when she got his message. We walked toward a quiet part of the terminal and Ameena called Mehdi back. She turned on the speaker phone when Mehdi picked up. Mehdi said that he recognized the man in the Kabul airport lounge. He said that he was always there.

"He is an old NDS guy nearing retirement. I suppose that's a soft dead-end job that none of the young agents wanted to do. He doesn't concern me. But I also sent the photos of the two men at the Bazaar to my field contacts. What I was told worries me," he said. "Your T2 was a KGB double-agent during my time in the Caspian. He did not transition to the FSB when the KGB was dismantled in 1991. Instead, he started working for Colonel Oleg, a former CIA Joint Task Force director," explained Mehdi. "Look, you may be in danger. Get Panther to tell you about Oleg. She will contact you soon. Be very careful," he warned.

I found Mehdi's news to be disconcerting. The biggest problem was that we had no idea what the threat landscape looked like. We had played this game before, but always within the realm of what is possible in Canada. I mean, I've dealt with North Korean and Chinese MSS agents, former KGB agents, Pakistani ISI, Indian RAW, even Sri Lankan SIS operatives. Nobody gets whacked over security matters in Canada. Out here in the open world, though, it seemed like peril lurked under every rock. Within a couple of minutes,

Ameena received a text from Panther. The message read, *Meet at Sendajski Garden by fountain, 1 hr. I'll find you.*

Ameena checked her map. "We need to hire a car," she said. "Taking public transit there will take us over two hours. It's only 44 minutes by private transport. Let's go."

C'MON, EILEEN

Ameena had already researched ride sharing in Minsk. In Belarus, among many former Soviet Republics, Uber merged into Yandex, a Moscow-based tech giant. She quickly created a Yandex account in English on her smart phone and used the credit card Mehdi provided. She ordered up a ride at the airport curbside. The app works in the same familiar way as Uber or Lyft. We got into the cab and headed into town.

Sendajski Garden was a small, unassuming green belt separating ministry buildings on one side and the Belarus State Academic Musical Theatre on the other. I imagined that this was a place for government workers to eat their lunch on sunny days. It was about a block from the Lenin Monument in Minsk. We pulled into the large parking lot off the Vulica Miasnikova entrance and got out. According to the GPS, the fountain was just around the trees. I looked around for other cars arriving but couldn't see anything of concern. We walked around the trees and found a shallow pond fed by five or six head sculptures from which two streams of water spouted into the pond. As we stood there, a little old lady approached wearing a knitted shawl. I almost walked past her when she whispered, "Ameena?" I was confused for a second. I gathered myself up when Ameena said, "Panther?" And the little old lady said, "Please, it's Eileen."

Eileen walked us over to the Belarusian State Pedagogical University across the Lenin Monument so that we could disappear in the underground parkade. There is a massive underground complex here. It is nearly impossible to hold surveillance and not expose yourself to your target. Like the Great Bazaar, there are just too many potential close encounters that inevitably end in a burn, unless the target is totally impervious to all activities in his or her surroundings. We walked toward a white panel van which Eileen unlocked with a key. She shoved us in the back where there were no side windows. When she jumped into the driver's seat, she removed her grey wig. It freaked me out, as I wasn't expecting it. She threw the shawl behind her seat and started backing up. While she didn't look quite as old as when we'd first seen her, she was not exactly spring chicken either.

"Stay out of view, we're going to a safe house to debrief," she said.

As we pulled on to the street, it occurred to me that 40 years ago, Eileen must have rocked. Here she was in her late sixties, and she was competent and relaxed about what she was doing as if she still did it every day. She did her heat checks, costume changes, and even a license plate change with utmost fluidity. That last change was performed in a residential underground with magnetic plates. There was even a dummy on the passenger seat that she propped up and down as necessary, and it had a flip-up reversible T-shirt.

We don't use such things at home. We're in a white, plain wrapper Ford Transit van. The city is littered with hundreds of these. There's one at every traffic light. It's like trying to follow a mid-90's Toyota Corolla in Vancouver. It's frustrating. Worse, some have license plates that are close in series to each other. So confirming your target by license plate at a distance won't reward you with any certainty until you have visually confirmed all six alphanumeric characters.

We drove into an underground parkade in the Kamennaya Gorka district in the north-west part of Minsk. It looked like a new development of residential high rises. The security in this building was tight. The parkade had two security gates that we fobbed through. The elevator lobby access from the parking garage required a fob, the elevator required a fob, and the second-floor unit required a key for the visible lock and a proximity powered transducer for the hidden magnetic lock that went around the entire door frame. Inside the safe house or apartment, it was as Plain-Jane as it gets. There was still an air of Perestroika lingering here, as if this structure had been a futile attempt to modernize the architecture. While the white walls looked clean and new, they looked shoddily finished. There were bulges in the middle of the wall—seemingly, an utter lack of attention to detail.

I turned to look at Eileen. Zager was her maiden name. She hailed from a Belarusian Jewish family. She was born here in Minsk in 1952 but travelled to New York when she turned 12. She lived with an uncle who operated a jewelry business in midtown Manhattan. She finished high school in NYC and took up Jewish Studies in the City College of New York. In her mid-20's she travelled to Israel and lived in a *kibbutz*. Then she returned to New York, became a US citizen, and sought a teaching job in Jewish history. She was later recruited by the CIA. She, like Mehdi and Nasser, started by working the aid NGOs. She worked in Asia with them, but when Mehdi and Nasser were hurled into the Stans, Eileen was sent to work the Arabian Peninsula. She worked directly under a man named Major Oleg. I wondered if that was the same Oleg that T2 in the Bazaar worked for. But why did they take interest in us? Was he related to the Stans supply group? Was he in the Saudi bureau?

Eileen explained that one of their unit tasks for the "grand plan" was to identify and select a core leadership that would espouse the new paradigm. The paradigm itself, codenamed "Operation Lancet," was a specific ideology that was to define their purpose, in the same way that a great corporate ideology is supposed to forge a single-mindedness that creates synergy and success. The goal was to recreate the Nazi ideology that had fueled the Third Reich and sowed the seeds of the Hitler youth. Then, step two: Weaponize the ideology. There was an extensive list of control methodologies brought into play: disinformation, polarization, marginalization, disenfranchise-ment, alienation, demoralization, and even psychosis, all leading to radicalization.

Eileen was a young fledgling analyst at that time. She basically did Major Oleg's bidding without question. Back then she did not have the faculties to question the CIA's motives. She was all in with Team America. Everyone was. They travelled all over the Middle East, drumming up anti-Soviet sentiment. They knew the Soviets were doing the same for America. It was like an ad promo campaign. They were far removed from the turmoil of the day, the OPEC crisis. At home in America, and in many places around the world, cars were lined up at the pumps. Fuel was being rationed. The ration coupons were being bought and sold on the black market. But Major Oleg and his AP team were only concerned with one thing—winning the Cold War.

They looked for natural charismatic leaders, people who could inspire and motivate multitudes. They wanted people from role model positions in life: doctors, academics, and maybe even celebrities and athletes who could move people's emotions. Jim Cunningham, Abubakhar Mehdi, Faizal Reza, and Nasser Tushanni were all assigned to cultivate operational networks in the Stans. Theirs was the unenviable task of recruiting the multitudes for the Messiah that both Major Oleg and Eileen were seeking. Eileen's team travelled all over the Islamic Mahgreb and the Arabian Peninsula talking to the political and clerical leadership to find someone who could be the focal point of an ideology, a rallying point of unity, and a voice to draw support for a new cause. What they were looking for was an ideologue, or maybe even a zealot—perhaps another Yasser Arafat, Fidel Castro, or even an Adolf Hitler. But this time, they would own him.

Major Oleg turned his attention to the Muslim Brotherhood, an organization whose leadership the CIA had been cultivating for years. Ultimately the team found a fringe group within that it could share common ground respective of the Soviet agenda. A partnership was struck. Now this was by no means a formal treaty entrenched in doctrines of sorts; all this was covert. The CIA was to provide the funding, the training, and the hardware. There was a need for tight choreography. Timing wise, they needed to be able to execute when they got the personnel on board.

The strategists determined that the ideological origin would be Salafist. And of course, it was no surprise that Ayman al-Zawahiri, the current leader of al-Qaeda, and Omar Abdel-Rahman, the blind sheikh who masterminded the 1993 attack on the World Trade Centre, were Salafist. There was one odd fellow that Eileen found right in the middle of the mix. He was a tall and lanky man with a zest for Wahhabism, a similarly conservative form of Islam. That fellow would later be one of the most uttered names in history: Osama bin Laden, a Saudi national related to the royal family.

Eileen said that by this time, Masub Tushanni was coordinating with the Pakistani ISI. She said that Masub and Nasser weren't really Pashtun, they were actually Baloch. But this part of Central Asia is all tribal; it made sense, at least to the CIA, to utilize an elder with Western education and a clear understanding of tribal structures and politics. So after Masub was turned from the KGB, he was relocated in Afghanistan. His job was to cultivate the Pashtun tribes, which later became the Taliban. Today, the Taliban is a much more diversified group; it had recruited Tajiks, Turkmen, and Uzbeks. But back in the early days, the Tajiks, Turkmen, Kyrgyz, and Uzbeks, republics located east of the Caspian, were all seeded separately. There was a need to keep their raison d'être religious as this was unlikely to change. They also knew from history that borders were of little consequence. Islam is one nation.

During the CIA's aid delivery in the Caspian, Mehdi would smuggle Crossbones into and out of the Stans. According to Eileen, Crossbones was Dr. John Marsdale, a biochemist who studied under Dr. Sidney Gottlieb. Eileen said that Crossbones was just an observer. She said that she had only seen Crossbones on their operating logs for the Caspian a few times. Otherwise, the operatives only knew he worked for a science program stateside. Major Oleg was always on the mission when Crossbones was around. They would be together in-station for weeks at a time.

Eileen said that she got out of the game during Operation Cyclone in 1979. She said that the complexion of the work had changed dramatically since the Soviets invaded Afghanistan. They had ceased the propaganda operations and the Agency then focused back on the cash management, the drug distribution, and arms supply. By late 1978 she could tell that there was going to be a ramp up of theatre operations. The signals and human intelligence ops continued in the Caspian, Black, and Baltic Seas, of course. The supply operations were like a production mill, supplying the *mujaheddin* with military hardware. The drug supply lines provided the cash, and overtly, the Carter administration rendered token amounts of money to the *mujaheddin*. These were the instances when one had to ask whether Jimmy Carter knew what was really going on. Or was that just an act to cover up any potential leakages in the future, part of some plausible deniability? Carter was pushing for more funds to go to support the *mujaheddin*; all the while, the CIA was pouring millions in through the backdoor.

The Department of Defense was fully cognizant of the potential to draw the Soviets into a quagmire, a Vietnam-type war that would profoundly engage Soviet resources for years to come. A comment attributed to a US DoD representative: "...the whole idea behind it was, should the Soviets invade this tar baby (Afghanistan), the US would want to make sure that they got stuck." *Seriously? Tar baby?* Not only did the US preempt the Soviets to invade Afghanistan, but this statement also shed light as to the value the DoD placed on the lives of Afghans and other "tar babies." And arguably, drawing the Soviets into a continuation of the proxy war in Vietnam was the objective, motivated by the profitability of war.

"But all that is already out there," Eileen said. "Just as we fabricated the circumstances to manipulate the 'gooks' to expend our ordinance in the name of freedom, we got these tar babies to fight a threat against their religion which did not exist.

"I was told that in Vietnam, where the people were poor, they targeted the farmers whose livelihoods depended on their ancestral lands. When the Soviets and the Viet Cong told the farmers that the US would take their ancestral lands, that's when the Cong started to fight for their lives. They otherwise had no reason to pick up a rifle. Land was the only thing they passed on to the next generation. If they had lost that land, they might as well be dead. So, they fought to the death. And they kicked the US' ass because they were more invested in that fight. The US was only there for the money, and worse, it was already dealing with fallout from eroding public confidence at home.

"I recruited Osama," Eileen stiffly admitted. "He wanted to come out and play."

As Eileen recalled it, Osama was not the man the media and the US had portrayed as a demon. She said that Osama was the modern-day Judas, and the propagation of Wahhabism was his 30 pieces of silver. But it was all a lie.

"I remember when I first brought him to meet Major Oleg. I flew him over from Riyadh at that time. Remember that we were looking for men to lead this crusade. Major Oleg must have envisioned a warrior type, like the brilliant strategist Saladin. Instead, I had this tall, lanky, quietly spoken gentle man standing in front of him. He shook hands with Major Oleg, and later, the major grumbled about the handshake being too soft. He said that Osama's hands were fucking softer than his wife's. He said he was effeminate. He called him a fucking fruit behind his back. And Major Oleg wasn't even sure if Osama was sincere. Oleg yelled at the team days later, asking if we could recruit people with spines.

But our recruits were the only ones who conformed to the desired profiles. We knew what we were doing. Osama was the one that others will follow. The selection from the Muslim Brotherhood was limited, leaning more toward the affluent; al-Zawahiri is a doctor, Abdel Rahman, our *zampolit*, was an academic. Osama came from royalty. And his thesis on the Quran's attitude toward its opponents in the perspective of Surah At-Tawba received international acclaim. We chose the best of the best. But Major Oleg was an abusive man; he would yell at these folks when he got impatient. And Osama would always respond so gently to him, and that incensed Oleg even more. I thought it was hilarious in the beginning—until I had just about enough of Major Oleg, because he was starting to get on my nerves. That Oleg was an ignorant motherfucker—please pardon my French," Eileen said.

I couldn't quite square up what I was hearing from her. Was the Osama Bin Laden she was describing the same man as the one I had seen on TV interviews, totting a Kalashnikov or an RPG-2, issuing *fatwas* and taunts against the US? Are we talking about the same bogeyman responsible for the most graphically horrific terrorist act against mankind, the same Bin Laden who had co-founded the Maktab al-Khidamat (MAK) alongside Abdullah Azzam?

"Yeah, Azzam was ours too," continued Eileen. "We yanked him in from the Muslim Brotherhood as well, that poor man. They killed him because he was too conservative for them. Abdi was also one of my recruits. They no longer wanted him. Abdi didn't believe in the whole global domination rhetoric of Islamic extremism. He was another one of those intelligent pragmatists, a great corporate man, but his vision was for the *people* of Islam, not necessarily for Islam itself. So they blew him up. Him and his two kids, while on their way to a mosque for evening prayers. I liked him. He was a good man." Eileen's eyes started to mist over.

"And the MAK. Did anyone seriously think they could have established themselves so quickly without the Agency?" said Eileen.

The MAK was the predecessor of al-Qaeda. It was a global logistics and financing operation for the Afghan war effort, the *mujaheddin*. Azzam was known as their promoter because he travelled all over to ask for monetary support for the *mujaheddin*. He went to mosques in Seattle, Sacramento, Los Angeles, and San Diego in the West Coast. He was all over the Eastern seaboard, and even central as well: New

York, St. Louis, and Kansas City. All told, they pushed him on to over 30 cities in the US alone. He toured more than Elvis ever did. Eileen said that she had never seen anyone work so hard. She was certain that his assassination was not MAK's doing. She didn't think that was an apt way for Major Oleg to deal with internal issues. "They were all honorable men," she said.

Osama inherited MAK after Azzam was killed at the end of 1989. Soon after, the movement simply became known as al-Qaeda, the base. That was the name they had used to cryptically refer to it from the beginning, when they did not have a colloquial name for the organization.

"It started as just a generic name, which referred to the logistics and planning group based in Afghanistan," Eileen said. "The base—and the name—just stuck. After the Soviets left, the mission of MAK was no longer the *root of schools,* which is what Maktab al-Khadamāt literally translated to. On top of that, the Afghan Services Bureau also ceased to exist. So, *al-Qaeda* it was."

"Who would benefit from killing Azzam?" I asked.

"Well, the organization evolved into something else after the Soviet collapse. There were thousands of people employed in the operations, both in theatre and back home in the States. Abdi became more vocal about his disagreements with Major Oleg. Maybe Oleg was afraid that Azzam was going to compromise the operations, or worse, expose it. So, who would benefit from his silence? Maybe Major Oleg or Masub, even Nasser. Masub and Nasser continued with their poppy fields and they're still at it today. It's been business as usual since the 70's, and they have amassed a tremendous amount of wealth pushing their heroin into the US. Remember that at least 95 percent of the world's heroine is supplied by them. It's mind-boggling."

"So how did your relationship with Osama Bin Laden end?" I asked Eileen.

"In the latter years, Oleg was ultimately his handler," said Eileen.

"I only recruited him, having established the initial rapport and vetting him. But then I no longer saw much of him after the Soviet invasion. He led the *mujaheddin* under instructions from Major Oleg. When I heard that al-Qaeda was responsible for the 911 attacks, at first I seriously doubted it. I was really disturbed by it."

Eileen took a deep breath. "Mehdi is dying. There are only a handful of people left alive who knew what it was like to be in Afghanistan during the pre-Soviet days. The system is replete with redundancies, multiple layers of plausible deniability built into the operations. There is no paper trail. There are no memos, no photos, and no recordings. The Agency relied almost entirely on heroin for financing. The ops were off the books, even the slush funds. There was no accountability to anyone.

"The warning bell has rung. They've killed Faizal. His body was so badly mangled they could only identify him by pieces of his clothing. It was really bad. I've never been frightened before in my life. But this story needs to be told. People have the right to know the truth.

"And when this gets out—" Eileen paused, her gaze becoming distant for a moment. Then she lifted her chin and looked me and Ameena straight in the eye. "They will come after me. I've thought about this long and hard for many years. Let it be," she said, resigned to her fate.

"Why would they kill Faizal?" I asked.

"We're not a hundred percent sure that it was because of Operation Cyclone," she said. "But years ago, during an argument with Major Oleg, Faizal mentioned that we had kept some of the operational material that we used, as a sort of insurance policy. They had their deniability and we needed to cover our own butts. I know that Osama was quite the packrat with these things. He hoarded documents that he was supposed to destroy. One night, one of Colonel Oleg's security details showed up in one of Nasser's camps. Osama was there with me at the time. I heard an argument about some manuals being outstanding and that they should have been destroyed. I was hearing this from a distance, and I wasn't paying real attention as to what the argument was about. I was more amused by the security guy yelling at Osama's interpreter while Osama himself had a big smile on his face. I hadn't thought about it in years. Now all of a sudden, it may have been important.

"Look, Mehdi and I have already discussed it. If people are out to get us, we're dead anyway. So we want you to be the vessel of an untold history. You are here so that you're not hearing it from a single source. Plus, there may be some retrievable artifacts out there. We never discussed who held on to what. But as a team, we learned about each other's habits, good and bad. I thought that when they went after Osama in 2011, they would go after us as well. We were nervous there for a while. But we knew why they went for him. Just the same way they went after Abdullah Azzam. They knew Osama had gotten tired of playing their game. The CIA wanted him finished. So they picked a good time to do him in. Obama's public opinion ratings had sunk to an all-time low. The military put a bug in Obama's ear that, quite conveniently, they had located Osama. Oleg might have manipulated the armed services to do his dirty job for him. Obama green lighted the mission. The rest is history. I don't intend to end up like him.

"Think about it, Osama had three wives and about two dozen children," Eileen continued. "Who's going to feed his family now that they've fallen into disfavour with the Saudi royal family? We thought they would go and kill Ayman al-Zawahiri as well. But they didn't. Maybe they're saving him up for something. And as for us, we've been out of Oleg's radar for years. Now, suddenly, we're running for our lives again. Well, Mehdi's done running. And I can't fight anymore. It's time that you took what we have and learn from it.

"So your next stop is Sudan. There is one more confession to hear. We decided all together that we have had blood on our hands for too many years. And many more continue to die, even today. We didn't expect, then, that technology would spread the infection far and wide.

Tomorrow, there will be even more. It needs to stop before it morphs into the evil of the End of Days. I don't know, maybe we're already too late," Eileen said. "ISIS is supposed to be no more. But the ideology spreads, like a virus. That is why it was named Operation Lancet. It was an inoculation. An ideological virus specifically engineered to repurpose and finally destroy its host. It is the weaponization of hate, making it one's reason to live, in order to bring death. The only way you can stop the dying is to expose the virus to sunlight. Show what it really is: a lie. It's just a big lie. We made it up. Tell them, those exposed to it, that they can't die for something we arbitrarily pulled out of our asses. We made that shit up.

"There is no time to waste now. They must already know that you are here," Eileen said.

"Who?" Ameena asked.

"*Them*, the cabal, maybe... Colonel Oleg, they're the only ones with anything to lose. Masub... Nasser," Eileen said.

"Nasser knows what we look like. We already met him," I said.

"Then you are already in danger," Eileen replied. "You see, a few months ago, we all met in Azerbaijan. We think that Oleg had us watched all these years. Maybe he suspected that something was up. That old fuck must have his paranoia dialed all the way to 10. Well, he drew first blood. Fuck him."

"What's Oleg been up to all these years?" asked Ameena.

"You know that Oleg contracted Adnan Khashoggi for that Iran-Contra Affair, the arms for hostages deal. Oliver North fronted the operation in public, but underneath it all was Oleg. Again, he was the overall architect of that exchange," said Eileen. "That is how Oleg got into the arms business himself. Oleg was behind Saddam Hussein's military incursion into Khūzestān, on the southern Iranian border, after the 1979 US Embassy hostage situation in Teheran. He sold those arms to Saddam and then double-ended the deal and sold arms to Iran so that it could defend itself against Iraq. What a fiasco. To keep Khashoggi out of contention, he later trumped up fraud charges against him, and that shoe lady, Imelda Marcos. Those charges went nowhere, but that's how Oleg ended up controlling the lion's share of arms deals on the planet. He is a much more powerful man now."

Just then, we heard a vehicle pulling up into the driveway below. Eileen opened a closet which housed security video surveillance monitors and she noted two men exiting a white landscaping truck. Each one retrieved a blue pelican case from the back of the truck before making their way to the front of the building. Eileen urged, "It's time to go."

She went into a closet in the hallway and dismounted three suppressed Heckler & Koch Maschinenpistole 5 submachine guns from the wall and passed two of them to Ameena and me. She had a couple of ammo go-bags and tossed them to us as well. The HK MP5 is an ancient weapon designed in the early 60's. Because it's been around for half a century, many agencies have trained their officers with them at one time or another. Ameena and I are among them. Having these HKs readily at hand felt like a reintroduction to an old friend. Ameena and I simultaneously checked the safety, racked a round into the chamber, and dropped the magazines for visual inspection. We extended the stocks and braced the weapons in the low-ready position. Like I said, it was an old friend.

"We're out of time," Eileen said. "You'll have to make it to Khartoum. The Tawhid Mosque on Tutti Island. The imam, Mukhtar al-Thaqafi. He was *mujaheddin*."

Eileen led us to a hidden hallway behind a false wall in a closet. She pulled out her cell phone and turned on the security app. The security monitoring was mirrored on her phone as we dashed down the escape tunnel. We passed the ground floor and exited through a utility door to a different parking garage from the one we'd driven into earlier. As we rounded the corner, Eileen pointed us to a silver Toyota Fortuner SUV and threw me the keys.

"You're 55 minutes from the airport. GPS in the car is pre-programmed. It's just the M9 ring road to the M2 and you're there.

Hurry, I'll hold them off."

But just then, a car exited the secured parkade and two men entered under the raised gate. They spotted Eileen on the opposite side of the car and started shooting at her. Eileen dropped down and crawled behind a nearby car for cover. The men did not see us behind the structural pillar and entered an open kill zone. But they came running at speed and were almost in point-blank range to finish off Eileen. I caught a glimpse of the fluorescent lamp on the parkade ceiling. This gave me distance bearings for the men when they cast their shadows from the lamp. I put my support hand on Ameena's right shoulder and raised two then three fingers to the side. This signified two targets at three meters. When Ameena nodded, we threw ourselves into barricade firing positions on opposite sides of our cover pillar. We executed two perfect head shots to the basal ganglia. Both men fell to the ground, dead before they hit the pavement. The ringing in my ears reminded me that this was no longer scenario practice. We had no ear defenders on. This was live. This was real.

Eileen got up from behind a car and said, "It's just a scratch. Go."

Ameena gave her a quick once-over to confirm that she was okay, and then she pushed me aside as she fired a shot at one of the men that we saw on the monitor taking pelican cases out of the landscaping truck. I thought that those were the men that we had just dispatched. There were two more. Ameena took out another and now there was only one left. I paralleled alongside a parkade wall, staying a full two feet away from it. I then noticed a suspended convex mirror, typical of parkades with sharp blind corners. I ducked behind a parked vehicle and kept myself very low. I just paid attention to the mirror for a few seconds. Sure enough, the second gunman slowly crept around the corner. When I saw him in the mirror, I sprayed four shots into the wall at a sharp angle. The bullets fragmented and continued to sail down parallel to the wall, hitting the last gunman in several places. He went down instantly, and I rushed him from cover, but it was a lost cause. A fragment had entered his right eye and ventilated his brain.

Now I was really pissed. I had to do some combat breathing to calm myself because I was so enraged. I instinctively wanted to do an administrative reload of my machine pistol. But I only recalled expending five rounds from what is a fifteen-round clip. Nonetheless, I took a spare mag out of my go bag and slipped it into my back pocket. Just in case. Ameena refused to leave until she was sure that Eileen was safe. She walked Eileen to the closest fire exit and sent her up the stairwell. Ameena came back to get me.

"Okay, let's go," she said. "Eileen says the first safe house was more like a decoy. There is a second one. It's armored and just a block away. She'll have her private security extract her later. Let's go."

A TACTICAL DRIVE
IN THE COUNTRY

Ameena took the wheel of the Fortuner. It was a midsize SUV not sold in North America but a big seller everywhere else in the world. To the uninitiated, it was the next size up from the 4runner, also built with a body-on-frame configuration. Here, it was powered by a 2.8 litre diesel engine. This was a workhorse of a truck. Ameena drove up the ramp to exit the parkade. Just when we got to street level, I noticed two more men in a white car pulling out behind us.

It was dark now and I couldn't identify the make of the vehicle. It followed us out to one of the main streets of the Kamennaya Gorka complex. Ameena was purposefully going slow to see if the car would pass us and go on its own merry way. But so far it stuck with us through two turns inside the complex. I turned on my Google Maps and the moment it started tracking us, I saw a narrow dead-end driveway heading east. I yelled, "Turn right, dead ender. Boot it!" As Ameena snapped the car right, she floored the throttle. This forced the following car's hand. The driver was dumb enough to expose his intentions, down into a dead ender no less. He started to chase us. This told me two things: first, he was the last car, no backups; and second, he was an idiot.

At the end of the driveway, Ameena put the binders on hard. "Evasive," I called out. The white car was following too closely and going too fast. So the driver had to hammer his brakes and go to our left side to avoid rear-ending us. The moment he paralleled us,

Ameena looked into the rear-view mirror and selected a point on the landscape. She then threw the SUV in reverse and throttled out to 60 kph going backwards. I watched her speedometer for her and called out the kph reading, "60." At that moment, I found the stability control button on the center dashboard and turned it off. She shuffle-steered the wheel left and let the weight of the engine rotate the front of the vehicle around clockwise. When the rotation passed the 90° angle, Ameena flipped the transmission back to drive and picked up the throttle as we sailed forward to the opposite end of the driveway. At the junction, I yelled, "South," and gave Ameena a distinct arm gesture left. I briefly looked behind and the white car was still trying to execute a five-point turn in the narrow chute of the dead-end driveway.

What Ameena pulled off was a textbook perfect flying-Y maneuver. It's an old stunt driving technique. The flying-Y and the slower speed reverse J-turn are executable evasive maneuvers in narrow confines. Done correctly, the vehicle is able switch directions a full 180°, within the vehicle's own length. The technique works easiest on vehicles with front engines, although it could be performed with vehicles of any configuration. The forward caster angles of the front wheels that self-centre the steering wheel and help the car track straight on the road have an opposite destabilizing effect when driving in reverse. Higher reversing speeds exacerbate this behavior. At 40 mph, the speed is sufficient that, with the help of the engine's weight, the vehicle's nose can be flung over until the reversing momentum is re-vectored to forward motion. The physics at play is similar to the tail-slide maneuver on aerobatic planes, only on a two-dimensional axis. The excess yaw is arrested by the driver's steering input, assisted by the caster angle grabbing purchase as the vehicle returns to forward travel. Done expertly, the transition is visibly fluid, and the vehicle doesn't shed speed through the transition. It is an effective anti-ambush tool. Ameena practiced the Y and J maneuvers often because, well, she liked them.

About 15 minutes into the drive, along the M9 near Baravaja, Ameena noticed a car closing in behind us at high speed. The car was in the fast lane and it slowed to parallel us. There were two men in the car, but we could barely make out their faces. It was the same white car we had evaded in Kamennaya Gorka. They must have guessed, correctly, that we were going to head for the airport. The driver swerved at us and forced Ameena onto the emergency shoulder. I could hear stones hitting under the right side of the Fortuner.

"Really?" Ameena said calmly. "You wanna play that game?"

I reached for my MP5 in the rear passenger foot well and brought it to a ready position below the window belt line.

"How do you want to do this?" I asked as Ameena accelerated. Speeds were building up now. "Keep it low," I said.

"Copy," Ameena replied.

"What do you think; can you pit from the right and hold it on a T?" I asked.

Ameena looked around her shoulder and her mirrors and said, "Waiting for traffic to clear."

The white car pulled alongside us again and started to move over. Ameena pulled back a few feet to match our front fender to the white car's right rear fender. When the white car moved over, Ameena changed into the fast lane, gently pushing out the white car's rear end until the passenger side of the car rested on our front bumper and grill. We were pushing the white car sideways at highway speeds. Its tires had stopped rotating and smoke from the skidding tires started trailing on either side of us. The wail from the tires was constant, and the smell of burnt rubber started to permeate our cabin. I saw the faces of two men illuminated by our headlights. I raised up my MP5 and fired through our own windshield. I saw the passenger's head explode in a red mist.

"Disengage," I said, and Ameena changed back to the slow lane.

This move released the white car and its front engine pulled its nose forward, going the same direction as before. Ameena accelerated away while I scoured for an alternate route. I don't think we had travelled more than a mile when I felt a surge and heard a loud thump in the back. There was the white car again, but this time it was rear-ending us. I saw bits of headlight and plastic parts from our Fortuner falling onto the roadway.

"I'm done with this guy," Ameena yelled.

I raised my MP5 and turned my shoulder around. Ameena put her hand on my shoulder to prevent me from turning around. "I got this," she said. She then accelerated the Fortuner to 180 kph, with the white car in hot pursuit. She went over to the fast lane and the white car followed in with us. There was a large lorry coming up on the slow lane. As soon as we passed the slower-moving lorry, Ameena slid back into the right lane, tapped the brakes for a second, and then mashed the gas pedal. The white car went sailing past us on the left, but Ameena caught right up to it again. She pitted the white car as before, but this time, she did not move into its lane; she only moved half a car's width into the fast lane—this kept the white car in a permanent sideslip. It was traveling in a 45° angle to the road, causing the rear tires to start to heat up and smoke again. The driver tried to accelerate away so that he could correct his slide, but as he accelerated, Ameena accelerated with him, maintaining the sideslip angle. By this time, the Fortuner's front left bumper had hooked into the right rear fender well of the white car. This was the optimum situation. Ameena had him exactly where she wanted him.

I glanced at the speedometer and read it aloud. "One-six-five," I yelled. Looking forward, I saw a broad bridge abutment approaching. "Three hundred meters," I called out.

"I see it," Ameena yelled back.

There was a concrete pillar about six meters from the left edge of the roadway. It was coming up fast. Ameena released the throttle slightly, allowing the white car to straighten out. Then all it took was a slight nudge of the right rear bumper, and the white car vectored toward the abutment. With its rear tires cooked, it could not regain control. The white car impacted the concrete bridge support and disintegrated. I could only see the initial impact as we drove past the abutment at speed. But judging by the size of the pieces of the car that bounced back on the roadway, there wasn't going to be much of it left.

Cops say it wrong all the time. Speed doesn't kill. It's the *difference* in speed that does. A hundred miles an hour to zero in no time against a barrier with no give—that's gonna leave a mark. I gave Ameena a high five and focused on navigating us to the M2 before someone else decided to take a pounce at us.

The rest of the ride to Minsk National was a thirty-minute eternity. We ditched the car and the weapons and ordered up tickets for Khartoum. We got flights on Belavia, a local airline, bound for Istanbul, and then bought continuing passage to Khartoum via Turkish. I had to buy more clothing because I had managed to get some blood on my sleeve (whose blood, I wasn't sure). While at the lounge, Ameena went online and Googled the names Dr. Sidney Gottlieb and Dr. John Marsdale.

She called me over to her terminal and said, "Look at this guy, this Dr. Sidney Gottlieb. I knew his name sounded familiar. Project MK Ultra. This is the same covert CIA project that I read about regarding the Allan Memorial Institute in Montreal. McGill University was even caught up in all that."

Project MK Ultra was a covert CIA-funded research program that studied mind control. The purpose of the project was to determine why POW's returning from the Korean War came home with displaced loyalties. Some prisoners had begun identifying with their captors. Many of the experiments included the use of psychoactive drugs like LSD and the full gamut of narcotics and opioids. The project involved 80 institutions, including respectable colleges, universities, hospitals, prisons, and pharmaceutical companies. It delved into the psychological effects of sleep deprivation, verbal abuse, and even sexual abuse. As was revealed in a Canadian class action suit, they apparently used electric shock convulsion therapy. There were many reports of unethical medical research, such as using unwitting test subjects, or paid prostitutes to drug their patrons, or record sexual encounters. Surviving records of MK Ultra were first declassified in 2001. But later, in 2018, a declassified document surfaced that described experiments with dogs that were made to run, turn, and stop by remotely controlling their brain implants. The exact breadth and spectrum of MK Ultra may never be known.

What's strange is that Dr. Gottlieb concluded his experiments, reported that they hadn't work, and then retired in an eco-balanced home in Virginia, where he raised animals, ate yogurt, and advocated for peace and environmentalism. Here was a scientist who had spent an entire career as a spymaster, a poison expert and a crafter of innovative assassination techniques. He headed the chemical division of the technical services staff, earning the nickname "Black Sorcerer."

Dr. John Marsdale, or Crossbones, on the other hand, was not named in MK Ultra. But he shared the same credentials and experience as Dr. Gottlieb. They were also close in age. It seemed safe to assume that Dr. Marsdale had been an associate of Gottlieb. Further, there were some innocuous documents that suggested that Dr. Marsdale had experimented with political and religious ideologies, research that closely aligned with the MK Ultra projects. I remembered what Mehdi had said, that this Dr. Marsdale would always be accompanied by Major Oleg and that they would spend a tremendous amount of their time in the Stans. This led me to suspect that MK Ultra had been implemented in the Stans.

Ameena seemed fairly certain that it had been. "It's obvious what Crossbones and Oleg were doing in the Stans. I looked at the Jonestown incident of 1978 for comparison. The People's Temple sect was established in 1955 in Indianapolis. It moved to California in the 60's and, in subsequent years, was implicated in the operations of the Mendocino State Mental Hospital," Ameena said.

"You're talking about the Jim Jones sect with the Kool Aid in

Guyana, right?" I asked.

"Yes," she confirmed. "Listen, there are a lot of publications about Jonestown being a CIA field experiment. That's all conspiracy theory baloney. I'm not concerned with implications; I am more interested in the viability of incidental learning from the Jonestown incident. What was learned and who learned it? Because the Jonestown control mechanisms parallel that of ISIS. Religious zealots so absorbed and so controlled by the ideology that with a modicum of physical force, their belief systems were able to defeat the strongest of all human instincts—that of self preservation and survival. MK Ultra was contemporaneous with the People's Temple. MK Ultra supposedly ended in 1967, or so they say. But by then, the control mechanisms were already hardwired into the brains of People's Temple members. So the People's Temple coexisting with MK Ultra on the same timeline is correlational. But if we can find an academic link between the two, then maybe we can find a causal relationship," Ameena concluded.

It was time to board. We were not expecting to be assaulted in the secured side of the airport, but with the people we were up against, that was not a sure bet. At least there were no outbound checks at the gate. Maybe the police had not yet processed what had happened in the parkade back at the Kamennaya Gorka complex, or the M9 near Baravaja. They probably thought they were two separate incidents and hadn't yet thought to lock down the airport and border points. I asked Ameena to message Panther to see if she had made it out okay. We sat down at the gate. The flight to Istanbul looked only half full, which was okay by me. Ameena got a response almost immediately. It said, *Got stitched up. Going to ground. Dropping phone. Good luck.*

"You better warn Mehdi," I said.

"I already did. No reply yet," she responded, sounding a bit worried. She said she wanted to advise Jabril that Mehdi may be in trouble. But she recalled Mehdi wanting to keep his favourite nephew out of it. And she wondered what good that would do right now.

We stayed on the secure side of the Istanbul airport when we switched planes. We wondered if the assassins sent to kill Eileen were initially unaware of us. We had so many unanswered questions. Why was the safe house attacked? Whose safe house was it? How did they know to track Eileen when she cleaned off so well? And why did Eileen, after so many years away from the game, need to have an escape plan? I reminded myself that in the cloak and dagger world, one was never certain where one's allegiances lie. What clued Major Oleg to start cleaning out skeletons from the closet? Had Mehdi and Eileen been straight with us?

There were still many missing pieces on this chessboard. Why would the MAK do the CIA's dirty work? What was in it for them? The Afghan Bureau was intrinsically a *de facto* resistance organization comprised of fighters from many nationalities whose only common-ality was religion. What would rally them to a single cause? I was inclined to think that money wasn't at the top of the incentive list. Would you try to sway Osama bin Laden with money? There had to be something in the offing. Not money. Not power: it wasn't like these clerics were megalomaniacs. Not nationalism: they were too ambivalent, and they were multinational. I couldn't see what possible carrot Major Oleg could have hung in front of them. There were no obvious desires in common between Bin Laden, al-Zawahiri, Abdul Raman, and others. What were the dominant themes within MAK's ideological spectrum at the time? Towards 9-11, they seemed to have been driven more by revenge. Okay, so let's work with that. Revenge for what?

As the plane lined up its final approach into Khartoum International, I thought about contingency plans. Of course, there was really only one plan, the one that would get both of us out of this alive. We'd scoped out where we needed to go, per Eileen's instruc-tions. At the moment, all our skin was in this game. And it could be a costly venture. I thought about going home. Not that I would ever abandon my partner, but it occurred to me that this was the first time during this trip that I had thought of home.

There was a bit of turbulence on the approach. I love turbulence, its like a gentle motion that rocks me to sleep. The tense stillness in the cabin allowed me a moment to doze off. As my mind emptied itself, I recalled that had this been a regular day at the office, I would've been home by 6 p.m. I would be greeted by Shintaro when I opened my front door. He would attack me as I came around the corner like Kato would Inspector Clouseau in *The Pink Panther*. Shintaro is my dog, a red and tan coloured miniature dachshund. I named him after the lead character of *The Samurai*, a Japanese television series from the 60's. Shintaro was an 18th century swordsman who protected the Shogun from his enemies, the black ninjas. Along with his faithful sidekick Tombei, a white ninja, he travelled the Japanese countryside invariably in search of a fight. Or maybe my memory was colored by the wishful musings of an eight-year-old with an overactive imagination. Its just the way I liked to remember it. They were like a modern police duo. I rarely remember my dreams. I likely relive a lot of traumatic events at night; events my mind refuses to migrate to my waking consciousness. I laughed in my sleep when I dreamt Ameena and I in the the roles of Shintaro and Tombei. Weird. The gong sound that accompanied the lighting of the fasten seatbelt sign awoke me from my stupor.

The drive to Tawhid Mosque on Tutti Island was only 21 minutes long (according to Google Maps), just over four miles. We could do this on foot if necessary. The problem was that the outside ground temperature was 107°F. I quickly glanced out the window when the pilot dipped the port side wing during the last maneuver. I saw that the runway looked like a black scarf laid out on a beach. We were landing in the middle of a desert. This whole place was the middle of a desert. I don't do hot very well. At least we still had some traditional clothing. *We'll change at the airport*, I thought. And that might throw off anyone looking for us.

We needed to split up, and then to join up later when the coast was clear. The advantage we were enjoying now was the fact that other people thought we were just cops who didn't know how to play this cloak and dagger game. We knew they had lots of experience and thought that they could run circles around us. Well, not today. Ameena and I can play this game too. *We may not be as good as them*, I thought, *but we're better than their expectations*. That may be all we'll need.

There were no issues at the passport checkpoint. Normally, going to different passport control lines risks red flagging vigilant authorities, if the manifest or ticket sales indicate that the pair had purchased their tickets as travelling companions. Customs officers are quick to use this indicator as grounds for secondary inspections. Also, drug traffickers will get their girlfriends or wives to carry their cell phones so that the information will not get captured at inspection. But, without a hitch, we successfully got out of the secured areas separately and decided to take separate cabs to the mosque. We departed five minutes apart, which was sufficient separation. Ameena spoke the local language, a variant of Arabic. And she knew how to behave and move like a local. So, from afar, she didn't look like a foreigner hailing a cab. I, on the other hand, needed to find a travelling group or family to shadow.

Finally settled into my own cab, I stared out the window and silently assessed our situation thus far and inventoried the many questions that still burned. Whoever these bad guys were, they had to be working for Major Oleg. He was the only remaining player with anything to lose if any of this information got out. His previous henchmen, Masub and Nasser, may have had an interest in helping him contain his secrets, but up to then, I hadn't seen a reason they would. Why would Oleg have waited so many years to kill off anyone who posed a potential threat to him? Why was he on the offensive now, so many years later? What else could he be protecting?

THE BROKEN PROMISE

Ameena was first to arrive at the Tawhid Mosque. I wasn't too far behind her.
Tutti Island is a delta where the White Nile and Blue Nile merge to
form the main Nile. It looks like a giant sandbar. The west side is like
a green belt, with grasslands and crop. The east side is comprised of
roads and building structures. I wondered if this mosque had a separate entrance for women. *No matter,* I thought, *they should all lead to the
same chamber inside.* It occurred to me that women are not obligated
to pray at the mosque. When they do, they are traditionally separated
from the men. Islam recognizes the special role of women in society
and therefore does not compel their attendance at a mosque due to
tasks like child rearing and homemaking.

I took my footwear off at the door. I looked around and saw
some shoe racks by the outer wall. We must have showed up between
prayer times because the racks were almost empty. I entered the
mosque with my right foot first. "*Asalaam alaikum*," I said as I entered
the mosque, although there was no one to greet me at the entrance.

The one thing to note when entering a mosque is to find the *qibla*
wall. There should be a niche carved into one of the inner walls to
denote the direction one faces during prayer. The key here is not to
sit with your toes pointed in that direction. Most people kneel facing
the *qibla*. Kneeling before it assures that one's toes will naturally point
toward the opposite direction.

At the opposite end of the main chamber, I saw Ameena wearing a veil, speaking to an old man. They whispered so as to not disturb the few worshipers in the prayer hall. As I walked over to them, I heard them speaking in Arabic. I repeated my greeting, "*Asalaam alaikum*." Mukhtar al-Thaqafi reached out to shake my hand, returning my greeting, "*Wa-Alaikum Salaam*." I shook Mukhtar's hand and then placed my palm over my heart. Mukhtar looked at me quizzically.

"Are you Muslim?" he asked.

"I am not," I replied.

"Ah, come. You are welcome." He then motioned us to follow him into his private office in the basement of the mosque. As I walked behind him, I noted that Mukhtar was a man of small stature. He looked about 75 years old, and probably weighed no more than 130 pounds. He walked with a limp on his right side. His arms were dotted with scars, and he had blotches of hair missing from the back of his head. He had burns on the back of his hands. These were old scars, I noted, likely decades old.

It occurred to me that this was the first *mujaheddin* fighter I had ever met. This is the real deal! These guys were from a bygone era. They were old warriors, like the Vietnam Vets. They lived and fought at a time when PTSD was unknown. I couldn't imagine what post-war meant for a *mujaheddin*. They did not exactly have a Veteran's Affairs to care for them. They were left flapping in the wind, discarded like an empty pack of cigarettes after the war was over. Mukhtar had that distant stare and sadness in his eyes. I've seen that look before. My great-uncle had that stare. He had fought with the USAF in the Far East (USAFFE). He fought under General MacArthur to retake the Philippines from the Japanese near the end of WWII. He saw some real horrors, you could tell. Mukhtar had that look too.

We sat on a rug around a small table in his office. A young boy came in. "*Salaam*," he said. Mukhtar introduced him as his grandson and asked the young boy for something. The young boy dutifully walked down the hallway to retrieve a pot of hot tea and put it on the table. Mukhtar thanked him and he left, closing the beaded curtains to give us some visual privacy.

Mukhtar spoke English like he had learned it from youth. Although heavily accented, his vocabulary betrayed his higher education. Ameena stared at the religious items on the walls and zeroed in on an old certificate. It looked to me like a diploma of some sort.

"You earned a doctorate in Islamic Studies," Ameena said.

"Yes, some years ago," Mukhtar responded. "If your parents could afford it, you were sent to Maddinah."

"*Qada' and Siyasah Shar'iyyah*," Ameena said. "Like our Governance and Law?"

"Yes," Mukhtar responded. Ameena and I glanced at each other briefly. I realized that we were in the presence of not just any imam; Mukhtar was a real scholar of the faith. Ameena just wanted to make sure I was on the same page as her.

We had never met a Sunni, specifically a *Salafist* of Mukhtar's education level in our line work. Most of the newly converted extremists we'd encountered were the wannabe-scholar types. This was part of that subculture. They just knew enough of the Quran to be dangerous, not just to others, but mostly to themselves. If anyone had the opportunity to read their blogs, often their academic discourse dissolved into a literal pissing contest. It turned into something like angry Jeopardy, based on who could quote the most scriptures out of rote memory. The problem was that most of their blogs were conducted in the absence of a moderator clergyman, so anything goes. Most of them don't even speak Arabic. It is all very much an amateur hour. Even a non-Muslim can see that it's all just pompousness, much to the consternation of actual, learned academics of Islamic Studies. But once those faulty interpretations get put out there, they gain a life of their own.

However, at the same time, there are those who manage to claw their way back from the rabbit hole of extremism. The story of Murad Storm Al-Denmarki, as he was known in al-Qaeda circles, is an example of a light twinkling at the end of a very long and dark tunnel. Storm was a Danish convert. Radicalized into the fold, he was well connected and well-placed in the organization. He was the friend of Anwar al-Awlaki, a Yemeni-American cleric who continued to radicalize individuals online many years after his death in 2011. Al-Awlaki was a great recruiter and motivator for the radical faith. Storm claimed that he actually delivered al-Awlaki his European bride, a blonde-haired and blue-eyed convert.

One day, Storm was engaged in a religious discourse with others in his circle when they came across a contradiction in the Quran. Not thinking this was ever possible, he conducted an online search for "Contradictions in the Quran," and ended up with a few hundred thousand hits. When Storm was done reading, he felt betrayed and manipulated. He turned against the institution he had supported for more than a decade. He ended up contacting no less than three security services, Danish (PET), MI5, and eventually, the CIA. Storm became a double agent. But the most significant thing he delivered was his old friend, Anwar al-Awlaki. Not long after Storm provided his coordinates, al-Awlaki became the first American citizen to be targeted by a US drone strike absent of "due process." This was an extrajudicial homicide which sent the think tanks reeling at potential global consequences.

After a comfortable pause, Mukhtar started. "I know why you are here. I was afraid it would come to this. I wondered how long it would take until they came for us."

I was about to ask who "they" were when Ameena tapped me on the knee, anticipating my question. *Okay, I get it.* Let's just let Mukhtar speak and get a pure version of his story without interruptions.

He said, "You have spoken to Abu—Mehdi— already, and then Eileen. The last chapter of this story is mine. It was not designed to be. I know what you are thinking: Why are you telling us this now? Well, the reason should become clear in the next few hours.

"There was a time when we thought that our secret was safe. We believed that, after a number of years, people would forget, and the world would move on. It is easy to move on—if one can walk away free of guilt. It is different for those of us who must bear the guilty burden of this betrayal.

"You know, we Muslims only ever wanted to live in peace. We've been defending our lands since the time of Muhammad, *alayhi salaam* (peace be upon him). Despite the rhetoric behind Salafism, Wahhabism, or even Sufism, each with its own flavour of ultraconservatism, the objective is always to find peace. This is peace for one's self and others. But it is the arrogance of man, and his thirst for power and wealth, that corrupted these wonderful doctrines. These men want to *be* Allah, not just follow Him through his prophet Muhammed, *alayhi salaam*. And they usurped the words of Allah to bend the will of man.

"Osama was my friend. He was a very nice man, loyal to his friends and a true scholar and servant of Allah. We joined the Muslim Brotherhood because we believed in self-determination. We were not so much anti-West as we were pro-Muslim. We believe that we, Muslims, have the right to be the best versions of ourselves without the distractions and impurities of the West. We have no cause to impose our beliefs on anyone; this was never the point. Islam is to be defended; it is not a tool for oppression. There were enough injustices being perpetrated on Muslim lands by Muslims themselves. We wanted to bring self-respect back to Muslims who have been ruled over by foreigners and enslaved, who have had their values and their interpretations of Allah's laws contaminated." Mukhtar spoke between slow, deliberate breaths.

"Osama was a gentle giant. He also had a giant heart. He had a soft voice and a disarming smile. He was like my little brother. And I loved him as if he was my own blood. I was a militant and he was a schoolboy. He was a dreamer. He shunned his family wealth to live as Mohammad, *alayhi salaam,* would have wanted him to. He thought that personal wealth was an impediment to truth. He shared what he had with everyone.

"I was teaching in Riyadh in the early 70's, when it all began.

Eileen came to me during a meeting with the Muslim Brotherhood. She said that she could help our cause. She said that there were battles that other Muslims were fighting around the world, but that these battles were being fought under an iron cloak so that the world would not see or hear their pain. She introduced me to Major Oleg. It was Oleg who promised that I would be one of the most significant Muslim leaders of this century. My own ambition and stupidity were responsible for the rest.

"This is how my own arrogance rewarded me," Mukhtar said as he rolled up his sleeves to display his scarred arms to us. "I have seen many battles. Many I won, and just as many, I lost." He continued to reveal different parts of his body, riddled with damage. He had punctures all over, slashes on his back, burns, shrapnel marks on his torso, and even bullet wounds in his upper thighs. Half the muscle of his right calf had been blown off. I had seen battle wounds before. I had seen many warriors. I had interviewed many suspected Tamil Tigers seeking refuge in Canada. But I had never seen a body so abused by war. It was a wonder that such a body had survived to tell its tale.

Mukhtar said that the CIA recruited him and many others to form subversive groups in the Stans. They planned most of their attacks inside Moscow proper, for impact. They knew that they would be calling the Soviets out for engagement in one of the republics. He said that in early 1977, he and several Uzbek operatives detonated three bombs inside Moscow. One was on board a train in the Metro. The second was in a grocery store near the KGB headquarters. The third blast was just meters away from the headquarters of the Communist Party of the Soviet Union. Of course, Mukhtar and his men did not claim responsibility for it. No one did. In its frustration, the KGB arrested and executed three Armenian nationalists for the bombings. Ironically, the Russian public blamed the KGB themselves for conducting the bombings. Mukhtar later learned that the KGB readied another three Armenians to execute should another attack occur, in order to dissuade further attacks. They would send a clear message: Perpetrators would always be caught.

Mukhtar, with CIA backing, planted the seeds for the Chechen resistance that followed in the late 90's and into the 2000s. But the Soviets also sponsored their own brand of political violence against the West in good measure. It was tit for tat. The Red Brigades in Italy and the German Red Army Faction were responsible for bank robberies, kidnapping, and sabotage. The Soviets wanted to use the left-wing groups to divide NATO by getting Italy and Germany to secede. I recall a book by an American author, Ronald Rychlak, who wrote that covert Soviet campaigns resulted in the hatred of Americans and Israelis by the Arabs and other Muslims elsewhere.

"Osama was a teenager then, and he looked to me for guidance over issues of politics and religion. He was still in school at the time, and I advised him to finish his schooling first because he would require knowledge to change the world. And he would need the credibility to lead our people. Al-Zawahiri agreed with me, and I think that is what ultimately swayed Osama to stay behind while we, the older gents, went to Afghanistan.

"But by 1980, Osama had completed his tuition and joined us in Afghanistan. Still in his 20's, he was full of life and ideals. He had no idea what the US would ask him to do in the following years," Mukhtar said.

By this time, a lot of my own mental images of Osama came to the forefront of my consciousness. I joined the National Security Program in hatred of this man. From 2001 onward, every NS investigator wanted to be the one to track Osama down and bring him to justice. For me personally, my energy to track him down was fueled by anger. It wasn't hatred because of 9-11 alone, but because he had single-handedly caused my life to change. In 2000, I was ready to leave my policing career. I had been disillusioned by many things— poor management, conflicting ideals, a fleeting sense of purpose— but as I set myself up to leave, 9-11 happened. It changed the state of global commerce so drastically that it became impossible to get my start-up business off the ground in Asia. So I joined national security to get at the bad guys responsible for that. And, over the years, I did get a few bad guys; but not the ones I really wanted. I, like everyone else, wanted Osama.

But by May 2011, it would no longer be possible. Under a blanket of darkness, a specialized armed unit of the US ended his life. And the hunt for bin Laden, which began in 1998 after the bombing of the USS Cole, ended abruptly. Instantly, he was gone. Suddenly, the world felt closure might finally be at hand. It was a feeling that was short lived.

"We conducted attacks in movie theatres, public parks, libraries, police stations, military installations, and embassies. The Soviets clamped down on the reporting of these events. But we weren't conducting terrorism in a traditional sense. We were engaged in guerrilla warfare. It's not the same," Mukhtar explained.

"Major Oleg once complained to us that none of the news agencies, not even the ones in the republics, were reporting any of the events. He thought that we might need to increase the scale of the tragedy we wrought on the Russians. So we recruited more and more local people in the Stans.

"Each one of us *imams* was provided with a purple book. It was our Quran, the one we taught in the special mosques, madrasas, and in the musallas. The document was authored by Dr. Marsdale. The purple book included instructions on the methods of recruitment, the doctrines we read, how often, and how we compelled the fighters to act. Some of the things we needed to do were to create a sense of displacement, isolation, despair, and moratorium, then rebirth to a renewed servitude to Allah. Step by step, the instructions laid it all out. The Communists only tolerated religious practices; they outright shunned public worship. The Communists became the enemy of Islam, and the rally point against whom we made the call for *jihad*.

"By 1979, as history recalls, the Soviets invaded Afghanistan. By then, the KGB had realized that all those attacks were not the work of the Armenians, but by Muslim dissidents from all over the republics, the Middle East, and central Asia. The KGB also realized that the CIA had been working in Afghanistan. Initially, their strategy was to implant a pro-Soviet communist government, the PDPA. I still think the KGB, through the PDPA party, were responsible for the assassination of Prime Minister Daoud Khan in 1978, during the revolution. But their efforts were too little, too late, in seizing political control of Afghanistan. In desperation the Soviets invaded Afghanistan. It was the only way to get at and destroy the terrorist camps that Masud and Nasser had built in the mountains. You see, the US propaganda campaign convinced the world that the Soviets were the aggressors, that they invaded Afghanistan for territorial expansion. It then consolidated support at home in the US. It was a convenient alliance between the CIA and the *mujaheddin* to repel the Soviets. Of course, the reality was very different. Al-Qaeda, or I should say, MAK, through its operatives in the Stans, reigned carnage on the Russian capital. They were able to do this for a couple of years before the KGB realized what was going on. We were the irritating boil on the side of the Great Russian Bear. We had money, of course; our operations were funded by the heroin Mehdi and Nasser transported from Pakistan. And the CIA routed the money to the defense contractors, who were always happy to deliver the weapons to us under the guise of aid. The ordinance was paid in full. It was quite the industry. The CIA surely knew how to create markets for arms manufacturers. The same C-130 transporters that delivered the heroin to the US also delivered the weapons on their return trip to the Razmak Valley in Pakistan. Mehdi trucked the weapons over the Khyber into Afghanistan, and onward to the Stans."

Then Mukhtar's tone became regretful. "I was young and foolish. Ambition and arrogance took me over. I was seduced by possibilities. I thought myself so fortunate to be given the opportunity to be of service to Islam. I had not a clue that I was about to be betrayed and that, in turn, I would betray my faith. I was Allah's proud warrior. I led many of the clandestine incursions into Moscow before the 1979 invasion. And when the Russians entered Afghanistan, I was there to repel them. Do you see my hands? These burns are from TATP. Yes, I was a bomb maker. But I could not just ask Mehdi for a cache of RDX, Semtex, or C4. Those have residue signatures. The attacks needed to appear homegrown. So we improvised. As you can tell, these chemicals were dangerous, unstable to handle. I have been shot many times. I do not even remember where all these scars are from. I limp because of a land mine; this burn is from a grenade, and I also fell from a cliff once. Another time I was in a cave when a Russian patrol flushed it with flames. It burned most of my exposed skin. *Inshallah*, some of my hair grew back. But through this, Allah did not martyr me. I wondered how I could be so unworthy.

"I travelled across the Arabian Peninsula and invited *mujahid* to come join *jihad*. They arrived in hoards. Young men, many young men. Masub and Nasser helped by ISI, brought the Taliban and later the Haqqani to the fight. We were all friends, old friends. Many young men died fighting. Two million Afghans died in that war. But I was not to be one of them."

Mukhtar then fell silent for a few minutes. We sat still, almost breathless, trying not to interrupt that silence. I tried to fathom the depths of Mukhtar's pain as we sipped our tea. I couldn't even begin to comprehend it.

"Osama, he was a person many *mujahid* followed. He was a gentle giant of a man. He spoke softly, but his spirit carried to the crowds. He was not a monster. But they turned him into one to suit their needs. He became what is known in your culture as the bogeyman. You see, Salafi people only want to follow the old path. They want to keep the faith pure by not allowing convenient modifications to Islam. It is like preempting the Sabbath in Christianity, where a mass heard on the eve of the Sabbath fulfills the obligation to hear mass on the Sabbath itself—just as an example. Salafism also reminds the believer that *jihad* must be observed and is of equal importance to the other four pillars of Islam: prayer, charity, fasting, and pilgrimage. But *jihad* was meant to be the *internal* struggle, a stage of growth in the faith. I spoke to a rabbi many years ago during my teaching years. And the rabbi said to me that he equates the concept of *jihad* to that of a developmental phase in psychoanalytic theory as described by James Marcia, a clinical psychologist. Marcia called it an identity moratorium, a phase in a process in which the individual consolidates components of his or her identity. The moratorium, he said, was the internal struggle to choose between which values to accept and which to reject during the formation of one's own personality. The rabbi said that *jihad* is the same struggle, in the practical interpretations of the tenets and doctrines of Islam. The Salafist will not accept this comparison because they are not equitable philosophical concepts in their eyes. In Sufism, the *nafs* is the closest in meaning to the word *self* or *ego*. But these are modernizations, not quite acceptable to the Salafi."

I was having difficulty reconciling this old, broken man in front of me with the image of the Muslim Brotherhood imam he painted for us with his tale. The CIA did recruit among the very best. And Osama was among them. They were probably some of the best clerical minds of their day, and not at all the black-and-white Machiavellians that they were made out to be.

"After ten years, the Soviets left. We had won. But it was at a tremendous cost. Oleg, the CIA, and the US did not hold up their end of the bargain. They discarded us like yesterday's newspaper, despite knowing of the many commitments we were forced to make in order to lure who was needed into our fight. We were forced to abandon those agreements, at great shame to ourselves and our integrity. What's worse is that they never even bothered to help us deconstruct the movement. So it evolved by itself, beyond anyone's control," Mukhtar said.

"Wait," Ameena said. "What do you mean 'deconstruct the movement'?"

"We created a weapon of our religion. Now there is a following, a false branch," Mukhtar replied.

"And what kind of compensation was promised? Mehdi, Eileen, and now you, speak of being betrayed. What do you mean by that?" asked Ameena.

"For us," Mukhtar replied, "it was a double-edged sword. We were betrayed by the Americans and, because of it, we in turn failed our own people. The promise must have been one of the most preposterous deceptions perpetrated by anyone, much less the CIA. They, through Oleg, promised us that they would urge the US government and the UN to support a return of the *Khorasan*. It would amalgamate the territories of most of the Stans under the rule of one *khalifa*. With the defeat of the Soviets and the disintegration of the Union, the republics would all be invited into the caliphate. At least, that was the vision. It was that dream that we sold to the *mujahid*. It was all a lie," Mukhtar said, his eyes tearing over. "We ... I ..." he continued, "sent many Muslims to their deaths. I pray that they all died *shahid*, even though their cause was not ever real."

Ameena and I were stunned. We're talking about our neighbours to the south, the US of A, our partners, with whom we shared the longest undefended border on Earth. It was *them*, their government? Or was it? Who did Major Oleg represent; was it the government, or some other authority with even more power within?

"A caliphate would have brought a unity to Islam that it had not seen in a millennium. It would have brought an end to many wars. It would have brought stability to poor African nations. It would have re-established old trade routes to South Asia and the Far East. And with diversity, we could all preach tolerance for the variances in our beliefs, Sunni, Shia, Sufi, Alawite, Salafi or Wahhabi, and yes, even Ismaili," said Mukhtar.

"What happened after the Soviets left?" asked Ameena.

"Osama and I argued with Oleg over keeping his promise. We suggested that he at least bring the matter for consideration before

Congress. But it became apparent that the whole incentive was a shallow sham. It was never part of a greater plan within the US government. It appeared that Oleg and his people had created the illusion on their own. Even today I am not sure if his superiors even knew about it. All they must have seen was money and weapons going to the *mujaheddin,* and saw that everything was going as planned, so they never bothered to ask the right questions, such as, *why would these 'tar babies' fight for America?* Well, they did not. They fought for themselves. Osama was very persistent and wanted to negotiate an alternate, maybe lesser, position that he could commit Oleg to. And that's when he laid his cards on the table," Mukhtar said.

"What do you mean?" asked Ameena.

"That's when they beat us," Mukhtar replied.

"*What?!*" I responded incredulously.

"Oleg and his men beat us. They broke my leg. My back was broken when somebody stomped on it with a heavy boot; I don't know who. This is why I am stooped over. My face was so bloodied that I could no longer see who was hitting me. Osama was tougher than any of us could have imagined. He took everything they had. They kicked him in the abdomen until he threw up. He bled from every orifice in his head. His jaw was broken, his cheekbones smashed, one of his eye sockets had to be rebuilt. They called us 'sand niggers.' After all that, all those years of service, this was all we were to them, fucking sand niggers. They dumped us outside one of Nasser's camps somewhere. I don't remember much of that day. Some medics found us and treated our injuries. But Osama had to come back to Khartoum to get his treatment. I thought he was going to die," Mukhtar said.

"Where was Nasser at the time?" I asked.

"He was there. But he neither said nor did anything to make them stop," replied Mukhtar. "They left us for dead. Osama was badly hurt…. badly hurt. That was the payment we got for being loyal, to our religion, to our people, and to America. Our reward was getting two million Muslims killed and being left for dead ourselves. *For what?* I asked—for heroin and arms deals, where they profited at both ends. These people are depraved. They have no respect for anything. Osama warned them that they would lose control over this ideology if they did not deprogram people. And he was right; as technology shrunk the Earth, the ideology took a life of its own. Modernization gave it momentum.

But Oleg, he did not care. His job was done. The cold war was over, the Union of Soviet Socialist Republics was history, and America had won."

My mind raced back to the first internal national security course I had ever taken. A CSIS dude spoke of what he called 'the worst intelligence failure in history.' He said it was the fact that the US did not realize that the reason the Soviets invaded Afghanistan was because they were already being hit by radicalized Muslims. Well, to the contrary, it turned out to have been the best intelligence ruse in history. Only a decade after the Soviets got drawn into the Afghan war, the East Berlin wall came crashing down. People only saw Reagan and Gorbachev as two proponents of peace on either side. But no one was held accountable for the blood that was shed in the conflict, blood that forced Gorbachev's hand. Two million Afghan civilians lost their lives, fifteen thousand Soviet troops, and no one knows how many *mujaheddin.*

It is true that *to the victors go the spoils.* And the victors also get to tell the story they choose. This turn of events now affords us the opportunity to right history, I thought, to somehow remedy the injustices that had been perpetrated on a generation of people because they had the softest voice in society. Because in their true religion—not the weaponized version—they are instructed by Mohammad to speak softly, be respectful, and only raise their voices when Islam itself is being threatened.

"Are there any of these purple books left in existence? I mean, these were tantamount to your operation manuals. And they must have been widely distributed back then," asked Ameena.

"They were secret documents. Only a handful of designated imams were permitted to study them. They were later collected by Dr. Marsdale after he completed an impact analysis on the ideology," said Mukhtar. Then he paused for a prolonged moment. It was as if he could not decide what to say next. "I am sure there may be a copy of it in our old mountain camp in Tora Bora, near where Nasser built his first camp. But the US Forces bombed those hills so intensively after 9-11 that the geography of the land changed beyond recognition. We could be digging for years."

"Yes, but you had lat/long coordinates of it, didn't you?" asked Ameena.

"We did. But I don't know who would have those now," he said. "What purpose would it serve now? That is what they killed Osama for," he added.

"What do you mean?" I asked.

"Osama vowed revenge. He thought of himself as a warrior then without a war. He had nowhere to go after we left Afghanistan in 1989. So he went home, only to find disfavour amongst his clan in Saudi Arabia. I'm sure Oleg had a hand in that as well. Oleg wanted Osama's influence neutralized. He wanted him excommunicated from the rest of the bin Laden family. He needed the rest of the bin Laden family for something else. So he concocted the story about Osama being upset about US Forces being near some of the holiest places in Saudi Arabia. He had just been beaten to within an inch of his life. He would be upset about any American for any matter. Contrary to what the US claimed, he couldn't care less about taking on Saddam Hussein for his invasion of Kuwait. That had nothing to do with Salafism or *jihad*. Osama was correct to see that as a matter of internal Muslim affairs. He saw the Americans as meddlers in those affairs. And he believed that the US was about to do what it had done to the Stans—the US was poised to break up the Muslim alliances. And he feared the US had Saudi Arabia's ear.

"So I invited bin Laden to come help me here in Sudan, my home. Here, he could rebuild his life, somewhat obscurely, at least for a while. Until he healed; until we all healed. I suggested that he continue to preach and write. So Osama complied and moved his families here. Many say he invested a lot of money into businesses here in Sudan. He left Saudi with his wealth and injected it into the Sudanese economy. But he did it hurriedly, and without any real investment plan. He tried to live here quite modestly. But in 1994, *takfiris* tried to assassinate him. Osama was angry. He was very angry and hurt. He blamed Oleg and the CIA, one and the same. He was sensitive, you know. He was hurt. And he vowed revenge.

"You see, through 1994, Osama believed that American interference with his family in Saudi Arabia caused him to be stripped of his citizenship. They also froze his assets. He knew Oleg and the CIA were afraid of what his assets could finance. The attempted assassination of Egyptian President Hosni Mubarak was also blamed on him. Such was the politics of the day. There were other viable suspects, like Hassan al-Turabi of the Muslim Brotherhood, but the Americans focused strictly on Osama. They loved applying the Osama theory to everything. *Osama, the Bogeyman*, don't you know?

"By 1996, Osama had worn his welcome here. Pressure from the US caused Sudan to expel him. So he took his three wives and children and went back to Afghanistan. Me, I found my peace here in Khartoum, this little island, this little mosque. I savour this little life, and its stark contrast to the grandeur ambitions and arrogance of my youth—the things that got me to Afghanistan. I have no use for power or material wealth. Those are mere temptations. They are what lead to impurities. Here, all I have is my practice of *sunnah*. It is enough."

"Is Sudan where Osama planned 9-11"? I asked.

"No, no, no. Not specifically. The first attacks against US interests came before that, in 1998. It was the bombing of the US embassies in Kenya and Tanzania. But here are where the complications lie. You see, although the Americans blame al-Qaeda for these attacks, the ideology is now in the open. No one owns it now. There is no longer any control of it. It is like cholera; it goes with the wind. I do not use Internet here, but I am told that messages similar to the purple book are widely distributed to anyone willing to take the time to read its contents," Mukhtar said. "Khalid Sheikh Mohammed, for example. They arrested him in Pakistan and charged him with masterminding the 9-11 attacks. America needed to find a scapegoat for the time being, and KSM was convenient at the time. He was a lower-level worker in Masud's group who was in charge of networking with the ISI. The 9-11 plan was an old concept developed in the early 90's. It was a simple plan, a Hail Mary attack, like in American football. The only thing complicated about it was whether the *shahid* could figure out how to fly the planes into the targets. Anything after that, a kindergarten schoolteacher could plan.

"When the FBI discovered Operation Bojinka in 1995, they saw the plans for the downing of multiple aircraft flying over the Pacific Ocean in one day. If I recall correctly, the plan called for as many as two dozen planes to be targeted over a 24-hour period. And this is just one example of purple book ideology running amok out in the world. Bojinka's key operative was that bumbling idiot Ramzi Yousef. You would remember that in 1993, he had Eyad Ismoil park a Ryder truck full of explosives under the World Trade Center. Yousef and KSM had an engineering report that mapped out the optimal place to park the truck, so that when it exploded, the tower would buckle under its own weight and initiate a cascade of structural failures that would have downed one building after another, like dominoes. From what I heard, the engineering report said that the blast would have liquefied the slurry walls that kept the water from the East River out of the foundations. To that end, a whole row of buildings would have collapsed into the Hudson. But these idiots, Yousef, Ismoil, Salameh, Ayyad, Abouhalima, and Ajaj, couldn't even get up early enough in the morning to do a job of that magnitude. They had been out partying the night before, drinking and carousing with women. By the time Ismoil got to the World Trade Center parkade the next day, the parking spot that he needed to park the truck in was already occupied. So these morons decided to simply park somewhere else instead, in an empty parking space on another level. The blast caused major damage, to the building and the mindset of New Yorkers. But they did no accomplish what they set out to do. The towers still stood. Unbelievably, Salameh went back to the truck rental place for a refund. That's how he was identified by the FBI. That was the first attack against the twin towers.

"You call it 'Amateur Hour', is that right? Aptly put," Mukhtar said sardonically. "KSM was no planner. So in 1995, he had the unfortunate experience of mentoring Ramzi Yousef, who partnered with Abdul Hakim Murad on the plot to assassinate the Pope during the papal visit to the Philippines. This plot was to be a diversion for the more grandeur Bojinka, which was supposed to start with 11 aircraft flying to or from the US to various points in Asia. Depending on the version of the story you've heard, of course, Murad inadvertently started a fire in the Manila apartment they had been renting under assumed names. They were mixing volatile chemicals, you see. The fire brigade was called out when the fire first sprang up, although the fire ended up putting itself out before they arrived. But both Yousef and Murad's first instinct were to flee from the apartment. The police showed up because of the smoke and found what looked to be bomb-making materials. When Murad returned to the apartment later in the day to fetch Yousef's laptop, he was met by a female police officer who pointed her gun at him. She fired a shot but missed him. Murad ran outside for his life and, in his haste, tripped over a tree root and was captured. Yousef and KSM got away, though. These guys were so inept that when they had signed up for the apartment rental, they asked the manager for a second set of forms because they had inadvertently filled out the original ones with their real names! I am not making this up."

"I remember that," I said. "And Yousef was arrested in Islamabad 23 days later. KSM wasn't arrested until 2003 in Rawalpindi, where both the CIA and ISI supposedly arrested him in a home with two other AQ extremists."

"Extremists?" Mukhtar repeated. "There were no extremists in that group. They were angry men who came in good faith and were betrayed. You don't have to be an extremist, or a Muslim for that matter, to want revenge against something like that. How do I tell Allah that I cost him two million followers to help infidels obtain that which He forbids? No one seems to phrase our dilemma in that context. Think of it: These men went into the mighty Soviet Union with sticks and stones and they brought down a mighty empire. You don't think that they could bring down the United States with a little help from its enemies? It can still be done, from within. Like a cancer."

"You said that the purple book is what got Osama killed?" Ameena asked.

"You know that Oleg and his agency have spies everywhere. And contrary to what the Americans have told the world, they always knew where Osama was after flushing him out of Tora Bora. How could they not know in which neighbourhoods to look? After all, the CIA created all of these neighbourhoods, all the networks, the Taliban and the Haqqani included. They taught the Taliban to plant the opium, the Haqqani how to move and hide the money inside of normal trading activity. The CIA established their connections to the global networks. Whose money do you think they first started to wash? The CIA knew everyone's moves. They knew Osama would escape through the Khyber and that they would not have the Pakistani Taliban's or the ISI's support to take him."

"So why didn't they kill bin Laden earlier?" I asked.

Mukhtar paused for a second. He took a breath and said, "You should know that Osama was a meticulous Muslim." Mukhtar's eyes welled with affection. "He was smart. He kept very detailed records of everything. He never destroyed any of the evidence like he was supposed to. He was a rat, I mean, you know, uh..." Mukhtar paused.

"Pack rat," Ameena and I said simultaneously.

"There seems to be a discrepancy with respect to the accounts of the raid in Abbottabad," I said. There was something else I suddenly remembered, and I forgot what I had just asked Mukhtar. "According to reports from the SEAL team, they seized bags of materials, documents, and all manners of portable electronic drives after they killed bin Laden. I am familiar with their work from their previously raids of terrorist strongholds all over Iraq and Afghanistan. And because of these raids, we learned what prodigious record keeping meant to Muslims. They collected incredible amounts of financial intelligence that eventually found their way to the think tanks and then, to me. That's how we learned the AQ financing typologies. But it's been nearly a decade since the raid in Abbottabad. And today, that intelligence product is still not available. Something is up."

"There is much for the CIA to want to keep close to their chest," said Mukhtar, not surprised. "I would speculate that if the information Osama kept ever got out, there would be significant repercussions. It would expose the real people of influence in Washington. The younger generation of Americans will likely disagree with the ethics and morality of their government's foreign policies, which were honed over the past centuries to service families of nameless and faceless elites."

What he said blew me away. Here was this diminutive cleric, a battle worn and scarred *mujaheddin* fighter living on the Nile Delta, who basically summed up what is wrong with the world today.

"Towards the end," Mukhtar went on, "Osama was tired of his exile. I was told that he threatened to expose the real objective of an operation he was placed in charge of. It was called Carbonite. I don't know whether he kept a copy of the purple book, but it was a detailed set of instructions on radicalization developed from MK Ultra. Mehdi must have told you about Dr. Marsdale. Marsdale used to make field trips to observe clerics trained by Osama conducting radicalization sessions. And the purple book contained the usurped quotations from the Quran, along with the desired interpretations. We radicalized elements within six former Soviet republics. But the CIA never cleaned up its mess. Oleg thought that when they stopped Operation Carbonite, the movement would die without clerics and funding. But he was wrong. We knew he was wrong that very moment. When we threatened to expose him for reneging on our agreement for political support for a caliphate, just like the US supported Israel, he had us beaten. Only then did we realize he had lied to us from the beginning. It was useless to raise the issue with anyone else. Osama wanted his revenge. He got it. And later, he paid for it, with his life. He was going to be killed anyway; it was just a matter of when it would be convenient for the US to kill him. And when the US needed an uplift—or maybe it was more the result of some political wrangling in Washington—the time came to notify President Obama that the military had found Osama. He was executed by executive order. Osama should pay for his sins, but our greater sin was the one against Muslims, not the one against Americans," Mukhtar said.

"I, too, will pay that price. I am condemned to it. The fact that you two are here today marks the beginning of my end. The only thing I care about now is my penance, for my share of those two million Muslim lives. *Inshallah*, Oleg will come for me. I am ready. I hope Mehdi and Eileen have made their peace. But I'm not just going to lie down. Oh, no. After all, I am Allah's warrior. I brought down the mighty Bear," Mukhtar declared.

In all the rush for Mukhtar to get his story out, we never got to tell Mukhtar what had happened in Minsk. When he mentioned Eileen, I realized it was the first time I had thought about her since we left Minsk. She said she was going to be okay.

Mukhtar bent down to read a text message that had just come through to his old analog Nokia phone (those are the safest kinds of phones nowadays). He stared at it in silence.

SHOWDOWN ON THE BLUE NILE

"They're coming. We need to get ready. I am sorry but I understand you both are capable warriors. We knew Oleg would come for us one day. And we are ready for him. Yes, I am still good for the game. You disrupted his operations, the one where the Baloch were killed, so you, too, have now become unexpected loose ends for Oleg. He is partnered with criminals now, the cartels in Latin America and Hezbollah Iran. He has been running his own program since he was released by the Agency. He needs to prove to the criminal organizations that he has the power to do what needs to be done. Don't forget that the Tushannis still work for him. They don't like exposure. Fail, and they kill you. That's what likely happened to the Baloch—they were dead anyway," Mukhtar said.

"Understand that you are now both in danger," he said. "You must keep moving. His henchman, Choudhry—do not underestimate that man's treachery," said Mukhtar as he started to lead us through some corridors under the mosque.

Mohammed Choudhry was the man who had arrived to Vancouver posing as Adham Baloch's father-in-law. *This story has now come full circle,* I thought. Choudhry must be running Afghan heroin through Balochistan into Iran. From there, Hezbollah moves the merchandise into Latin America. And the revenues from the tri-border regions of Argentina, Brazil, and Paraguay are amalgamated in Venezuela and moved through offshore banks in the Caribbean. These revenues are then siphoned into numbered company accounts and sent to Iran via Dubai, Abu Dhabi, Doha, London, Paris, Vancouver, Toronto, Seychelles, and Singapore, to name a few intermediaries.

We must have stumbled into Oleg's MDMA operations. He sourced the precursor chemicals in Canada and the Baloch brothers delivered them to the Vancouver clan lab groups associated to Hezbollah. The police kept calling them Middle Eastern Organized Crime groups (MEOC), a name that exposes how little the police actually understood about these transnational criminal organizations.

But right now, we had bigger things to worry about here on Tutti Island. There is one bridge at the southern tip of the island. It is the only way in and out of the place. It's a deathtrap. It was time to convert that disadvantage into an advantage. And Ameena and I had already thought about escape routes during our flight here.

Luckily, Mukhtar had lived at the Tutti mosque for over 30 years. He knew the island intimately. Better yet, he knew people at the east bank of the Blue Nile.

"We'll boat our way across if we have to," Mukhtar said.

Khartoum North lies to the east of Tutti island, across the Blue Nile. There is farmland on the other bank, and just over a mile further east is a rail system. Covering all exit points off this island would require a lot of personnel. Let's hope that Oleg won't have that many, I thought.

Mukhtar led us into a storage area under the mosque where they stored copies of the Quran. Mukhtar opened a wooden door and pulled out a wooden box that looked like an ordinance cache. He took out a couple of AK-47s with folding stocks, one for each of us. He passed out double magazines strapped together in opposing orientation; one 30-round banana clip attached to another upside down one. These 60 rounds weighed a ton. Mukhtar decided he would take a 30-06 rifle with a scope instead. Although we never trained with AKs, I knew that these rifles were conceived by the Kalashnikov design team to be purely intuitive. These were the rifles the Soviets supplied to conscripts and farmers alike, with the intention of nearly zero orientation time with the weapon before pushing them into combat. They have a well-earned rugged reputation stemming from the Vietnam War. Sour grapes on the opposing side rumoured that the rifles were inaccurate and clunky. But anyone who conducted empirical tests with the weapon was surprised how wrong those misconceptions were. And the rifle's design allowed the weapon to fire effectively with minimal maintenance. I have seen how brutally effective the 7.62 x 39 mm round is, against steel or human flesh, and everything in between. I had walked up to remnants of American tanks displayed around the Cu Chi Tunnels in Ho Chi Minh City, formerly Saigon. There, I saw the armor deeply scoured by these rounds. Poachers in Africa kill everything with this round, from elephants and rhinos to crocs. I was certainly happy to have it by my side that day, rather than some 9mm pea shooter.

I watched Ameena, whom I knew to have never handled an AK before, load the magazine front lip, then back. She discovered the mag release as the rear lip seated. She naturally lifted her left hand over the top of the rifle, reached for the charge lever, and racked a round into the chamber. Then her right hand's middle finger swept over the safety lever and she was ready to roll. The AK is pure genius for design, even today—especially today.

Mukhtar gave out burlap bags to conceal our weapons in and led us out the east door of the mosque into a residential alleyway. He gave us canteens of water as we popped out the door. I could immediately feel the heat of the sun. It must have been 120°F by then. It was like Death Valley outside of Las Vegas in the summer. We hoofed it over to the water's edge to the east. By the time we reached the water, two Toyota Land Cruisers pulled up from the road. From a distance, I could see two men alight from the first truck and three from the second. They were all armed with submachine guns. They started down the steep bank towards the water.

There was a sand bar on the Blue Nile side of the island that grew with the receding tide. At the narrowest point between Tutti Island and the sandbar, it was about eight feet across. There had been a pile driven into the sand so people could use it as a step to traverse over to the sandbar, which was connected by land to the southern tip of the island where the bridge was. Mukhtar was no longer able to move as quickly. Although we had a few hundred yards on Oleg's men, they were catching up to us.

The sand bar was flat and featureless. There was no cover to be had, only distance. With our AK's we had the advantage, providing we still had distance. Mukhtar paused for a second and looked towards the men.

"That is Oleg himself, with Choudhry and Nasser. I don't know who the other two are. But it will be a fair fight," Mukhtar said.

I didn't know what his concept of a fair fight was, but we were in retreat. Then I recalled a quote: If you find yourself in a fair fight, you didn't plan your mission properly. We needed to find the upper hand.

Ameena yelled at me to slow Oleg and his men down somewhat. I took my rifle out of the burlap bag and positioned myself on a contour in the sand. I filled the burlap with hot sand and benched my position in. From a distance, I fired rounds at the men to prevent them from stepping on the pile to cross the narrows. I only squeezed out single shots to save ammo. But the men dove into the slow-moving water and below my horizon to cross to the sandbar. I knew that if they surfaced on my side, I would fall into a disadvantage. I looked towards Ameena and saw that she and Mukhtar had made it more than halfway down the sandbar. She motioned me over and I ran south to her location. Ameena positioned herself in a depression for cover as Mukhtar continued towards the bridge.

As I ran, I could hear bullets zinging around me. Ameena began firing from her position as Oleg and his men ran towards us. I ran past Ameena's position and caught up with Mukhtar as he pointed me up the bridge abutment. I turned as I heard Ameena squeeze off another round and when I looked back, one of the men dropped to the ground. Great, I thought. That's four against three. I ran up to the level of the bridge deck. It was an elevated position that I could fire down from. I laid down suppressive fire as Ameena ran towards the bridge. She caught up with Mukhtar, who was slow to get up to bridge deck level. But eventually, they made it up to the roadway.

We moved further south towards 56th Street and the modern Corinthia Hotel on the other end of the bridge. At mid-span, two of the men had caught up and were coming towards us, spraying bullets all around us. I was thankful that they had brought burp guns, the type where you spray and pray (pray that you actually hit something). They're excellent for close quarter firefights, in which machine pistols have proven their worth. But over distance, they have the accuracy of a one-eyed gnat.

I wondered where the other two had gone, and what fate had befallen the one that Ameena had shot.

It was tough pushing Mukhtar with any turn of speed. The two men were quickly gaining on us. A spray of bullets later, Mukhtar caught one in his right thigh and he went down. I crouched to reduce my target profile and returned fire, but the men were able to deke behind the side crash barriers on the bridge. Those just deflected my rounds further downrange. As Ameena helped Mukhtar up, one of the men jumped on to the roadway and fired a prolonged series of shots.

Just then, a white panel truck flew past us and struck the shooter with such impact that he flew 15 feet in the air and landed on the other side of the crash barricades. Three people got out of the panel truck. It was Mehdi, Nurab, and Eileen. Eileen was still bandaged up, but she had a pistol concealed in her sling and a riot shotgun.

There was no time for pleasantries. The two Toyotas were back, Oleg and Nasser each behind a wheel. They stopped just north of mid-span. They both got out and took cover behind Oleg's vehicle, which was in front. We all retreated behind the panel truck. But now we had shots coming in from two different directions. I caught a glimpse of a shooter who ran through the sandbar with the now deceased guy that Nurab had hit with the van. It was Choudhry. And he smiled when he saw my surprise. He popped his head over the barrier a second too long and Ameena blew his head off, shooting through the smashed windshield of the truck. The next spray of bullets from the Toyotas struck Nurab in the shoulder. The next bursts struck me in the lower left side of my torso. I fell as I reeled in pain from the burn of the bullet. But it was a through and through wound. I thought it might have caught mostly fat because there was hardly any blood. Body fat usually plugs bullet holes.

As I lay on the ground, I could see the legs of people around me. A third vehicle pulled up behind the Toyotas. The driver surely saw the shooting and was avoiding crossing into the line of fire. Oleg got into his truck and started it up. He turned the wheels toward the centre of the road and accelerated. The truck jumped the median and rammed the front of the panel van, sending Ameena, Mehdi, Nurab and Eileen flying backwards. Nurab, who was standing by the right front fender, was thrown clear to the other side of the crash barrier. Ameena got up and jumped over the crash barrier for cover. Mehdi and Eileen were flung hard against the barriers and knocked unconscious as they fell to the ground. They were both badly stunned and lay motionless.

Oleg emerged from the wreck of his own vehicle, bloodied and staggering. He pulled out a MAC-10. I crawled from underneath the panel truck to see where Nasser had gone. I lost track of Nasser when I went down. The last time I saw him was when he started shooting from the second Toyota. I couldn't see where he had moved to. Just then, Nasser suddenly appeared on top off me, pistol in hand. He pointed at me very quickly and I stared down the barrel of his gun, unable to move. Then I looked him straight in the eye, in time to see his head snap backwards in a mist of blood. I recognized the rifle report, which was an AK. I turned my head to see that Ameena had taken a benched shot on the barricade, taking Nasser squarely between the upper lip and the tip of the nose. Nasser dropped to the ground instantly. Before he hit the ground, I managed to nudge forward to get a better view of Oleg.

Oleg walked around the front of the panel truck towards Mehdi and Eileen, who were still dazed. I grabbed my AK-47, but the stock had unfolded, and it was jammed underneath the front tire of the panel van. It got lodged underneath when Oleg rammed the vehicle. I had no weapon. Ameena was behind the crash barrier and could not see Oleg pointing his pistol at Mehdi. I tried to find something to throw or distract Oleg with, but there was nothing else around. I saw Mukhtar lying on the ground. He was likely unconscious from losing blood. But his weapon was on the other side of him. I couldn't see it and I could not get to it in time. I saw Ameena slowly move north behind the barrier, looking for Oleg. But Oleg was now standing on top of Mehdi and Eileen, ready to shoot point blank, execution style.

Oleg wiped the blood dripping over his left eye, and as he lowered his left arm, he extended the right hand that held the MAC-10. Then a shot rang out from the distance, hitting Oleg in the back. He briefly turned around to see the shooter. I couldn't see where the shot had come from either. I was still on the ground.

Oleg looked incredulous about getting shot. I slowly pulled myself up from the ground to see Oleg shoot at the vehicle that had parked behind Nasser's Toyota. He sprayed a dozen rounds in one burst. I could hear the energy of the bullets impacting and ricocheting off automotive gauge steel. Oleg quickly turned back towards Mehdi and Eileen, intent on finishing the job. But at that moment, Ameena emerged from the barrier and pumped two shots into Oleg's chest. I could see the bullets take two chunks of flesh and propel them backward through the exit points. And before he fell to the ground, another shot fired from the third vehicle, penetrating the back of Oleg's head and propelling him down on top of Mehdi. Regaining his senses, Mehdi pushed Oleg off himself and away from Eileen. Then he sat up and looked towards the third vehicle behind Nasser's.

The vehicle door opened slowly, and a man I had never seen before emerged. He was wounded. He had been hit on the left arm and was bleeding from the face. He shook off shards of glass from his shirt and walked towards Mehdi. By this time, Ameena had climbed over the barrier and was by Mehdi's side. As the man approached, Ameena began raising the muzzle of her AK-47, but Mehdi raised his hand, motioning for her to lower her weapon. I stepped in front of the panel van to see the man approach.

"Are you alright, Uncle Abu?" Ameena asked.

"Meet Faizal," Mehdi said. "An old friend from my days in the Caspian Sea. He just happened to come back from the dead; just now. To help an old dying friend live a few more months."

Ameena gave him a wary nod, and then walked over to Mukhtar to help him up, leaning him gently against the barrier.

"I am sorry I am late, Abu," said Faizal Reza. "It did not help to keep myself out of the brew for so many years. He blew up my car anyway. Son of a bitch." Faizal turned to look at Oleg's lifeless body.

I remembered then who he was. Faizal, he was the Central Asian handler for both Mehdi and Nasser.

Faisal took both of Eileen's hands and pulled her up to a sitting position. Then he turned to Ameena. "Salaam," he offered. By this time, the Khartoum police had arrived, as well as ambulance services. Two of the ambulance workers rendered assistance to Mukhtar first. He looked old and frail as he sat up, clutching his side.

I turned to Mehdi and said, "I think I could use some of that Kalash whiskey now."

He smiled and said, "There is one last bottle in the truck." I thought he was kidding until Faizal fished it out of the passenger door bin. He took the cap off the bottle, took a swig, and then passed the bottle to me. Aren't there any traditionalists among these guys? I guess everyone drinks.

I did not have to use Mehdi's credit card this time. As I was being treated at the hospital, the RCMP liaison officer stationed at Rabat, Morocco, checked up on me and Ameena, to make sure we were okay. He said Ottawa told him that this was the first time in Canada's 150-year history that Mounties had gone on a rogue mission. After we went dark in Islamabad, our headquarters put a notice out with the Hague to coordinate an emergency extraction plan. He said that the Islamabad LO was genuinely worried.

"Oh. And he was plenty pissed too," the Rabat LO added.

After ending my call to Lorne, I turned to Ameena. "Where's Mukhtar?"

"The next wing," she said. "He's going to make it. He's a tough old bugger. One of the doctors knew him. She had apparently known him for years. She treated many of his old wounds. While he was getting stitched up, the doc turned to me and said, 'Come Armageddon, only Mukhtar and cockroaches will be left on Earth.' They're still laughing back there."

I checked on Mukhtar that afternoon. He was in good spirits. "*Inshallah*, I am still here," he said. He pointed out that in his younger day, he was more agile and feisty. He would have taken Oleg's men head on – all of them. I'm sure he would have too. I'm doubly sure that he's done that kind of thing many times.

I thanked Mukhtar for his wisdom and asked him what he was going to do next. He said that his life had always been here in Khartoum. He needed his mosque and its people needed him. Here, he said, is where Allah had ordered his penance. I bade him farewell and cupped his hand before turning towards the door.

"*Asalaam alaikum*," Mukhtar said.

"*Wa-alaikum-salaam*," I responded, and then I walked out.

The following day, as we readied to depart the hospital for the Khartoum airport, a new white panel van emerged on the driveway. Nurab was driving it. He had a thick wad of bandages on his shoulder. And I could see Mehdi, Eileen, and Faizal.

Mehdi stepped out of the front passenger side of the van. He slowly put a foot down on the curb and walked over to us. He put his arms around me, patted me on the nape, and then did the same with Ameena. Nurab came around the back of the van and retrieved a large black pelican case and handed it to Ameena.

"This is what Oleg came for. Osama kept a copy of his files here in Khartoum. He entrusted it to Mukhtar. And only Mukhtar knew where it was hidden. It was behind the wall of a neighbouring mosque. The imam there is an old friend. Mukhtar asked me to give it to you. This will rewrite history as it has been told. Do with it what justice must. We are not its deserving guardians. Not anymore. It is not everything of what was in Abbottabad. But it is most of it. It is enough," he said.

"The purple book?" Ameena asked.

"Yes, photographs of every page. This version is in Arabic. The texts were later translated to the native languages of the Stans," Mehdi said. "Ledgers, bank accounts, NGOs, numbered companies, voice recordings, waybills, fake passports, and even loadmasters' notes and payload manifests of those C-130s. Everything you need to tell the story is here. You know, Oleg never knew for certain whether there was a copy. But he had to suspect it existed when he realized you made your way to Minsk to see Eileen. He could not risk dismissing the possibility," Mehdi continued. "Ultimately, he felt that the three of us communicating again was no coincidence. His people got careless. They did not confirm that the body in the wreckage was actually Faizal."

We accepted the pelican case with some trepidation. We said our farewells, and promised to keep in touch. Mehdi instructed Nurab to drive us to the airport, and the three old friends turned towards the hospital to check on Mukhtar.

Ameena and I flew back to Vancouver with the pelican case in tow. I had the drives sent to the forensic technical crime unit for preservation, but more importantly, to gather up the terrorist finance information. After all, that's what Ameena and I do for a living. This information will bump our expertise in the world of global terrorist resourcing to new heights. It was a gold mine of information. Apparently, Osama had demanded meticulous detail from his operatives. I suppose he kept records to protect himself as well. Sadly, this was a lesson learned during a very dark time in the history of mankind.

I thought of how far this trip had taken us, both literally and figuratively. How strange is it that one of the most important things in the fight against terrorism is the definition of what a terrorist is, and we take it for granted We are all programmed to hate the bogeyman. It's easy to hate a stranger. It's the story of the Frankenstein monster retold. But now terrorism, to me, has a face. And it's not what I expected it to look like. The lines between right and wrong, between good and evil, are blurred, often beyond recognition.

They say that what you feel about something changes the moment your perception of it changes. It is normal to get angry at someone for speeding and driving like an idiot, until you learn that he was actually rushing to the hospital because his newborn had stopped breathing. Anger turns to sympathy instantaneously. There was a time when I was so sure of my own convictions, my sense of righteousness. But it is true that one man's freedom fighter is another man's terrorist. I am perceived as a freedom fighter in my own line of work—but perhaps I, too, am someone else's terrorist. Is there a place on Earth where I would be scorned as an oppressor? Where are the real bad guys?

Yes, Osama should have paid for taking more than three thousand lives that day. Are those lives more valuable than the two million lives the Afghans and *mujaheddin* lost? Did one single individual even have to die? And for what? Make your judgement as your God will judge you. So, before you do, make sure you have the facts right.

I remember that shortly after 9-11, a media commentator weighed America's options: Would it seek revenge on the terrorists, or turn the other cheek? *Turn the other cheek*, I thought, *what a repulsive concept.* Because back then, I had no idea that, someday, we would actually get to slay the beast. Only the beast turned out to be an image of ourselves in the mirror. It was just us. We were the terrorists all along.

BACK TO ONE WORLD

I went back to the 9-11 memorial in New York just this spring. The last time I was in NYC, the museum was still a few days from its inauguration, so I did not get to see it. I recall the twin towers fondly. I went there a few times in the 70's and 80's. My uncle had an office on the 86th floor of the south tower. I remember watching the bicentennial fireworks show over the east river from that office. It was a magnificent view. In its place now is the new One World Trade Centre, standing majestically against a cloudless sky. It stands testament to a nation's resolve to rebuild, to reacquire, and reinvigorate that which was lost.

A museum now occupies the bowels of the former twin towers. The museum pays homage to the men, women, and children who perished during the attack of September 11, 2001, as well as the prior attack that occurred on February 26, 1993. Its planners did well to focus on the victims and not the terrorism. It shines the light on what was good amid the darkness that befell ground zero for many years. The museum highlighted the heroism of emergency services personnel, but there were also countless accounts of civilians selflessly helping others. There were many heroes that day. Not all of them wore uniforms.

I stepped into the Memorial Hall, 70 feet below street level, under what would have been the footprint of the south tower. In the hall were walls dedicated to photographs of the thousands of people who were lost that day. They were victims of the WTC collapse, the attack on the Pentagon, and the crash of flight UA93 in Somerset County, Pennsylvania. I stood in the hall alone for what seemed like an hour. In the stillness of my mind, I wasn't alone. As my eyes panned across the many photographs of faces that dignified those walls, I was overwhelmed by an eerie energy. Looking at the faces on the walls, trying to get a sense of who they were, what their lives were like before 9-11, I wondered what it would be like to talk to them, if they were alive today. At that moment, the artifacts became more than just photographs on a wall. I heard their voices. They cried for justice; they cried for truth. They wanted me to write this story. They wanted the scales of blind justice to benefit all equally: Muslims, Christians, Jews, Buddhists, atheists, and everyone in between. *Write the story*, the voices said in unison. Write the true story.

I don't believe in the existence of an omnipotent secret sect whose hand controls governments and economies. But the analyst in me can't ignore indicators that suggest that its existence is more than plausible. For as long as governments keep secrets and maintain covert accounts, there will be open invitations for dark shadowy people to capitalize on the absence of accountability and unchecked power. Power corrupts, and absolute power corrupts absolutely. It is human nature. How could Major Oleg, a single man, have been the focal point of so much death and destruction? Who did he represent? He possessed so much power, yet he was no more than a low-rung henchman serving very well-placed masters. Yet he too was expendable—the likes of him always are. The two million Muslims, thirty-five thousand Soviets, and, more recently, eight thousand American soldiers in Iraq, couldn't have been expendable. Or were they? Were they just pawns in a game played by superpowers? Like a game of thrones?

Today, this viral radical ideology had seeped into the lowest denominators and most vulnerable layers of our society: the disenfranchised, the marginalized, and the mentally ill. For many of them, this ideology is an out. Like the devil, it beckons. *Everything will be okay*, it says. *Everything will be fixed*, it promises. *You only have to die*, it entices. *You will be rewarded*, it fibs. They're still dying today. They will continue to die until we recognize that this is everyone's problem. Not the military, not the police—ours.

Be assured that there really is a solution. We need to expose the deception. We need to inoculate the next generation from this madness. Immunization can only be achieved through education and having resources allocated for the affected. They say that sunlight is the best disinfectant. This is me pulling up the shades.

George W. Bush once said, "If I didn't think it was necessary for the security of the country, I wouldn't put our kids in harm's way." This tells me that even the president had no concept of what covert America had been up to. Were these lives really the price of freedom? Or were they simply the cost of doing business? Who profited? Who had motives and opportunities? *Follow the money*. This is not rocket science, folks. It had always only been about money and power.

Recently, unconfirmed reports circulated in the media that Hamza bin Laden, son of Osama bin Laden, was killed during an air strike. It apparently happened some time ago. The intel was picked up through chatter among extremists. True or not, I can't possibly imagine the kind of upbringing Hamza had. He had no choice, life afforded him no options. No one is born with hatred. It is taught. Terrorism used to be something that happened halfway across the world. Today it's at our doorstep. The last four terrorism incidents in Canada were attributable to recent converts, zealots. Neither the police nor the military are equipped to end terrorism. Society needs to hit the stop button in the terrorism production mill. Today, terrorists don't come from somewhere else—we breed them right here at home. The stop button is on the wall of your home.

I am retiring at the end of this year. One thing I've learned from a career in anti-terrorism is that the answer is not more bullets. In

Colombia, it was open hearts, the acknowledgement of grievances, and a countenance of reconciliation that brought FARC fighters out of the jungles and back to their families. I am hopeful that this generation we call millennials is well equipped for the task. I hope they break the cycle of narcissism and glean the lessons learned from my generation's failures. I hope they will be kinder and gentler to their own.

Please remind them, in case they forget, what "One World" always stood for.

In homage to all who fought and died for their families,
their communities and their countries,
no matter whose side of the conflict, anywhere in the world.

Peace be upon you. Asalaam alaikum

ABOUT THE AUTHOR

Archie Alafriz retired a 27-year veteran of the RCMP. He served more than half of his career as a threat finance specialist in the National Security Program. There, he enjoyed many successes in the anti-terrorism front. His first novel is a fiction based on the best plausible game theory analysis of the events that led to 9-11. He explains how "false" realities and storylines are created as a matter of tradecraft; oftentimes for political purposes. To label someone a terrorist dehumanizes them, he says. The label places limits to our perception and prevents us from seeing the marginalized, the disenfranchised and mentally compromised. Archie wrote this story in hopes of diminishing our fears and opening our hearts to compassion. It's hard to believe, he says, that halfway around the world a child lays awake at night, in fear that we may come for him or his parents. Today, Archie is a consultant for anti-money laundering and terrorist financing based in Vancouver, Canada.

CPSIA information can be obtained
at www.ICGtesting.com
Printed in the USA
BVHW030139110920
588550BV00001B/53

9 781525 568541